Ten Thousand Truths

Susan White

The Acorn Press
Charlottetown
2012

McDonald International School
144 NE 54th Street
Seattle WA 98105

Text © 2012 by Susan White

All rights reserved. No part of this publication may be reproduced, stored in a retrieval system, or transmitted, in any form or by any means, without the prior written permission of the publisher or, in case of photocopying or other reprographic copying, a licence from the Canadian Copyright Licensing Agency.

ACORNPRESS

P.O. Box 22024
Charlottetown, Prince Edward Island
C1A 9J2
acornpresscanada.com

All rights reserved
Designed by Matt Reid
Printed in Canada

Library and Archives Canada Cataloguing in Publication

White, Susan, 1956-
    Ten thousand truths / Susan White.

Also issued in electronic format.

ISBN 978-1-894838-83-2

    I. Title.

PS8645.H5467T45 2012   jC813'.6   C2012-904339-7

Canada Council   Conseil des Arts
for the Arts   du Canada

The publisher acknowledges the support of the Government of Canada through the Canada Book Fund of the Department of Canadian Heritage for our publishing activities. We also acknowledge the support of the Canada Council for the Arts for our publishing program.

To the courage and resilience of Jason Verner, Jodie McCluskey, and Travis Boyer. I consider myself privileged to have been a small part of your lives.

There are joys which long to be ours. God sends ten thousand truths, which come about us like little birds seeking inlet; but we are shut up to them, and so they bring us nothing, but sit and sing awhile upon the roof, and then fly away.

—Henry Ward Beecher

Chapter 1
If Not for a Pack of Gum

Rachel had just intended to grab a pack of Juicy Fruit and head down to the ball field. Margaret had told her she could have half an hour to hang out before she had to be back home.

A new foster kid was coming today and Mrs. Thompson would be bringing her at six o'clock. Rachel was supposed to be back in time to peel the potatoes and help set the stage for the performance—the one that would see Margaret Harriet and her husband, Bob, play-acting the roles of loving and caring foster parents. The props would all be set in their places: the chore charts would be on the fridge, the smiley face name tags would be stuck over the coat hooks at the back door, the place would be spotless, and Margaret would make sure that Bob was sober.

This new kid would make five foster children for the Harriets. Five little darlings that nobody wanted. Five little projects for Margaret to gush over when anyone from Social Services was around. Five little incomes. Rachel would have to share her room with this new girl, for a while anyway. Rachel had seen many kids come and go. This one would be no different—just a little hitch in the smooth running of the Harriet household. And Rachel had that down pat. She knew if she played the good little foster daughter when necessary, the Harriets would leave her free to do what she wanted. Knowing all the Harriets' best-kept secrets didn't hurt, either. Best kept, or their foster kids would be taken away from them, their monthly paycheques would stop coming, and Bob might actually have to get off his butt and get a job.

It had been a whole month since Rachel had been allowed out anywhere except to go to school. When Mrs. Thompson had brought Rachel home from the police station four weeks ago, after the breaking-and-entering incident, she'd suggested that Margaret ground her, and then gradually allow her more freedom until she could prove that she understood the consequences of her actions. Up until that incident, most of the trouble Rachel had caused was at school and it hadn't really bothered Margaret that much, except for the nuisance of having to put on a good show for the principal and pretend she had real concern for Rachel.

It hadn't been hard to break into the house. Once Rachel noticed that the window by the back door had been left open a bit, it had been easy to squeeze her arm through and unlock the door. She was never planning on stealing anything. She'd just wanted to stay there for the night. She knew that the family wouldn't be home for a few days. She'd watched as they'd packed their van and chatted excitedly about their trip to Prince Edward Island.

Rachel had actually been watching the family for a long time. There was a mom, a dad, a girl about her age, and a boy a couple of years younger. They had moved into that yellow house about six months after she had arrived at the Harriets'. Watching them had become an obsession to her. She walked by that house every day on her way to and from school, and sometimes she'd sit on the fence across the street, just watching them. She didn't know their last name, but she knew the girl was Emma and the boy was Daniel. She loved hearing the mother calling their names when she came to the door to call them in from the yard. She had seen the dad sitting on the front step one day, drinking a bottle of Alpine beer. The little girl had been drawing on the paved driveway with a rainbow of coloured chalk. The chalk had faded out over the next couple of days, and when she'd walked by three days later, the colours had washed away completely.

It was just a little pack of gum. No big deal. She had pulled off much bigger victories than that. Like the time she went into the store four times in a row to lift something, just to prove to herself that she could. Four times in a row and four different items, ranging from a tiny box of Tic Tacs to a can of apple juice. The store owners, Mr. Goodinsky and his half-deaf wife, never suspected a thing. She went into that store at least a couple of times every day and she always managed to get a bonus item or two.

But somehow she got caught this time. Mr. Goodinsky stopped her as she headed out the door and totally freaked out when he found the gum in her pocket. He started screaming at her and telling her he'd had enough of punk kids coming into the store and stealing from him. Rachel tried to make a run for it but he grabbed her and pulled her back inside. His wife had had to stop him from totally losing it. Apparently that little pack of gum was the straw that broke the camel's back, so to speak.

By the time the cops had come and picked her up, it happened that Rachel and the two police officers arrived at the Harriets' house just as Mrs. Thompson and the new foster kid were walking up to the front door.

"I can't believe it!" Margaret screamed when she opened the

door and saw Rachel, her uniformed escorts, the new foster child, and Sarah Thompson all squeezed into her small front porch. "In trouble again, and after all we have done for her? I really thought after the police were involved last time that we had gotten through to her on the importance of making good decisions. Today was her first day out since her arrest and here she is in custody again. I can't take any more of it!"

To add to the drama of the moment Margaret started gushing over the new kid, hugging her to her massive bosom while hollering to Bob to come out and get the suitcase Mrs. Thompson was holding. He was, of course, sitting in front of the TV, too caught up in "Wheel of Fortune" to be the least bit aware of what was going on at the front door.

"You have to take Rachel out of here *now*!" Margaret screeched at Mrs. Thompson. Her body blocked the door as if she were afraid Rachel would force her way in and her very presence in the house would contaminate them all. "I refuse to have her in my home for one more minute."

Rachel knew that a trade was being made: a new, good kid for her, an old one that was cursed and evil. She was sure that if Margaret could twitch her nose and spout some secret chant she would use her powers to make her disappear into thin air, instantly eliminating the problem and every memory of Rachel Garnham ever having been in her home. *If only it were that easy to wipe away the memories of living in this house for the last three years,* Rachel thought to herself.

Rachel sat on the garbage bin, still guarded by the two officers as if she was a threat to the very security of the whole street. Margaret let Mrs. Thompson squeeze by her so she could go upstairs and pack a few things in Rachel's backpack. While they waited for her to return, Margaret stood in the doorway, keeping her eyes and ears on Rachel as if afraid that at any time she would start spouting stories that would make the authorities think twice about leaving small animals, let alone children, with her and Bob.

The ringing of the phone startled Amelia. The fact that the phone rarely rang along with the early hour made the shrill sound even more jarring to the quietness of her kitchen, where she stood in the dim light ready to strike the match to get the day's fire going in the wood cookstove. Chelsea had had a bad dream last night and her screams had woken Amelia at about 3:00. It took over an hour to settle her and get her calmed down enough so that she could fall back to sleep. The kids were all still sleeping and Amelia rushed to the phone, hoping it hadn't woken them up.

Sarah Thompson was on the line and by the sound of her voice and the time of day Amelia knew she was calling to tell her that she was bringing her another child. She listened while Mrs. Thompson listed off the information about the girl she was bringing: Rachel Garnham, thirteen years old, five years in the system after losing her mother and brother in a motor vehicle accident. No father in the picture and no family except an estranged grandmother. Some behaviour problems, a recent break-and-enter charge, and a shoplifting incident.

Amelia liked Mrs. Thompson, certainly better than some of the social workers she had dealt with over the last thirty years. Some of them had treated her like she was a feature in a circus sideshow. *Come see the crazy, deformed woman who never leaves her tent!* They were happy to leave their problem children with her but they never took the time or effort to understand who she was or what she worked so hard to provide in this "last resort" place where they had been dropping kids off for all those years.

Mrs. Thompson came more often than some of the others to follow up on the kids she had brought to Amelia. It had been her who had brought Chelsea and Crystal to Amelia's four years ago, when the only sounds that came from them were the frantic cries they made if anyone came near as they clung desperately to each other. Mrs. Thompson had come regularly enough to see their language develop and their security issues improve to the point where they were able to go to school and be apart from each other for short periods of time. She hadn't been there, of course, for the day-to-day work that had been done to get them where they were now, but she always offered any support she could give.

Rachel had never seen or been on a ferry. She didn't even know there was such a thing around here. *Haven't these people ever heard of bridges?* she wondered to herself as a fat guy with a huge fluorescent vest waved them up the middle aisle of the maroon-and-white barge and Mrs. Thompson stopped the car up against an orange pylon. *That pylon wouldn't stop anything,* thought Rachel. *If Mrs. Thompson hit the gas instead of the brake, the car would hit the ramp and drive off into the water ahead. Now that would maybe make this stupid day something to remember.*

"Do you want to get out and look at the scenery?" Mrs. Thompson asked, as if the two of them were out for a Sunday drive.

Rachel's grunt and her slouched body answered loud and clear that she wasn't the least bit interested in looking at the trees, the blue water, or the high hills framing the river. One thing she knew was that wherever she was going, it was out in the middle of nowhere. No convenience stores in sight. She figured that was one of the main reasons they were making her come here; the philosophy like the one that would recommend keeping a drunk away from a bar or a fat guy away from KFC. Lakes, rivers, trees. Just what she wanted: the excitement of nothing in the middle of nowhere.

They turned left after getting off the ferry and drove up a curving road with a steep cliff wall on the passenger's side. Rachel watched a rush of water gushing down the side of the rock face. The river wound as far as she could see out the driver's side window. She stared at it until they came to the top of a hill and the road turned away from the blue expanse of water.

A brown church sat off to the left, surrounded on two sides by a fenced-in graveyard. For a second Rachel thought of that other graveyard, the one where her mother and brother were buried. Even though she had only been back there that one time, when her so-called grandmother took her there a week after the funeral, she remembered it clearly. She remembered standing there staring at the ground where just days before her mother and brother's caskets had been lowered in holes under those two mounds of dirt. How could two small mounds of dirt be the only sign of the deep holes where she knew her mom and brother were now? She hadn't really even been able to say goodbye that day because her grandmother had hurried her back to the car.

Mrs. Thompson turned at a sign that read Walton Lake Road. She slowed right down to 20 kph as the narrow road was dirt and very rough, which just seemed to make the drive more painful and foreboding. Rachel had no idea what to expect. Her mind kept telling her she was going to a place from which she would never return—she would spend her life trapped in this forsaken place and no one would hear from her again.

As they drove down the winding road, Rachel noticed a house with a green roof up on the hill to their left. *Maybe I could go there for help if I'm able to escape,* she thought to herself as they passed the mailbox. She wasn't able to make out the faded name on the old, rusted metal.

They continued through thick stands of trees until they came to the openness of a large lake. They drove the length of the lake and turned onto a long, even rougher driveway that was barely wide enough for the car to get through without hitting the bushes lining both sides. At the end of the driveway there was an open field with a house on one side. Most of the paint had chipped off of the once-white house, leaving it a dull grey with only a few small flakes of the white paint remaining. Several sheds with the same mottled look stood beside the house. The hill a ways over to the right of the house sloped down toward the lake they had passed on the way in. In the other directions all Rachel could see were trees.

After the car came to a stop, Rachel opened her door, slowly put her right foot on the hard-packed ground, and reluctantly stepped out. She saw a woman come out the screen door and step onto the veranda of the old house. The first thing Rachel noticed about the woman was her face—it was like the surface of the moon. Warts, moles, or bumps of some kind stuck out from her chin, her nose, and her forehead. As the woman walked toward the car, Rachel saw nothing else but the warts and she didn't hear the woman's first name when Mrs. Thompson introduced them.

Rachel heard the wart-face saying something about the history of sneakers: first produced in the year 1800; called sneakers because the soles were smooth and made no sound on the ground. Rachel looked down at her feet. The day after her eviction, when Mrs. Thompson got back from picking up the rest of her stuff, Rachel had been relieved to see her orange High-Top Converse sneakers sticking out of the box. Her lucky sneakers were the only thing she cared about in that box of crap. Maybe if she had been wearing them on the day she got caught shoplifting she would have had better luck. She had worn them the night she had broken into that house, and even though she had gotten caught she had been lucky enough to get away with staying there all one night and part of the next day. Long enough to form a clear picture of every room in the house so that she could put herself back there in her mind any time she wanted to and pretend it was her house and her family. If she conjured up a pretend family she wouldn't have to remember the family she lost and all the fake families she had been forced to live with ever since.

"You are about a size 6, I would guess." The warty woman's voice broke through Rachel's thoughts. "Did you know that in 1324 the King of England decreed that barleycorn would be used as a unit of measurement for shoe size? Three barleycorns—which is just a grain of barley, I don't know where the corn part comes from—laid end to end is about 1 inch. An average man's shoe size is 33 barleycorns, or size 11. A size 6 would be 18 barleycorns. Are those beautiful orange sneakers 18 barleycorns?"

Rachel didn't know what to say to this grotesque woman, who was obviously certifiably insane—so she just shot her a dirty look and reached into the car to pull out her stuff. *Warty*, Rachel thought. *They are dumping me here in the middle of nowhere with Crazy Warty Walton.*

After Mrs. Thompson drove away, Rachel picked up her backpack, a garbage bag full of clothes, and one large Rubbermaid container containing the rest of her worldly possessions and followed Amelia into the house. The first room they came to was the kitchen and it looked to Rachel like something off the set of the *Little House on the Prairie* movies she had watched non-stop when she was a kid. The main feature in the room was a big woodstove covered in steaming pots. The heat of the kitchen felt suffocating. *It's August, for God's sake,* Rachel thought to herself. *Why do they need a fire in the middle of summer?*

The look on their faces is always the same when they first arrive, Amelia Walton thought as she moved a large boiling pot toward the back of the stove. Everyone always looked for a second or two too long at her face. She sometimes forgot herself, what her face looked like until an accidental glimpse in the small rectangular mirror hanging over the bathroom sink would remind her. She usually felt like she was still her twenty-year-old self when the only things on her face were a couple of light brown marks.

Rachel shifted her backpack, set the garbage bag on top of the container, and followed Amelia through a wooden door beside the kitchen sink and up a steep staircase to a landing where an old sewing machine sat under a small window. From the window Rachel could see some bushes behind the house. Three heads were sticking up out of the greenery.

"This is your room," Amelia said as she opened the door at the top of the stairs and led Rachel into a bedroom. "You get your own staircase right to the kitchen and the biggest and warmest bedroom in the house. This was my bedroom when I was a little girl. Believe you me, you will be glad for this room in January. This old house is not insulated very well and it can get pretty cold in the wintertime. The stove you saw downstairs and the old wood furnace in the basement are how we heat this house. The chimney comes up through here as you can see and you'll be surprised at how much heat will come off of those bricks when the fire is going well. It will be your job to keep the fire going on cold nights since you have the back stairs outside your door. Don't worry—I look after the furnace. It is old and temperamental and likes to be loaded just so or it won't give a bit of heat. Zac keeps telling me I am going to have to break down and put in a new one. He says a new model would give out more BTUs. That stands for British Thermal Units which is a unit of energy needed to heat one pound of water, one degree Fahrenheit. That old thing has been warming this house for as long as I can remember and I can't see any reason why it won't keep doing it for as many winters as I have left. I just tell Zac he has to be more selective in the wood he cuts me. The old thing has a preference for maple and a bit of hemlock and if you give him that he gives back plenty of BTUs."

Rachel had no idea what Amelia was talking about. She was still stuck on the fact that she would have to keep the fire going. Not only had she been dropped into this other world, with a crazy lady who didn't seem to stop talking, but she had been pushed back a couple of centuries. *Is there even electricity here?* she wondered.

The light bulb sticking out from a white socket on the wall answered that question for her. There was a little chain hanging down from the socket. The two windows in the room gave enough light so there was no need to pull that chain to see if it actually worked. *This is going to be like being in some kind of country bed-and-breakfast jail,* Rachel thought to herself.

"The other kids are out picking raspberries. Zac will come by tomorrow morning and get whatever they pick today and take them to the Farmers' Market and sell them for us. With the few strawberries we have, along with the raspberries, the eggs, the chickens and turkeys, and the vegetables from our garden we do pretty good this time of year. You're lucky you came today. It's grocery day. Zac buys surprise treats for the kids every week but believe me they don't last long. Just leave your box and bags here on the floor. You can unpack later. Let's get you outside to meet the kids, the dogs, and the other beasts that make up this funny farm. Oh, I'll show you where the bathroom is first. You probably need to go after that long drive from Saint John. The toilet is a bit finicky. During World War II a German submarine was sunk due to a malfunction of the toilet. No fear of that, though, that flood last week was a bit of a nuisance."

Rachel considered her options as she sat on the toilet. If she tried to run away, she wasn't sure she'd even remember the way back to the ferry. But if she did get that far, she knew she could walk to the highway and probably hitchhike her way back to the city.

Rachel hadn't even seen a phone here yet. There was that house with the green roof they had passed, Rachel remembered. The people who lived there probably had a phone—if she ran away from here, maybe she could go there. But who would she call? She remembered her grandmother's phone number, but she doubted Hilda Garnham would even remember she had a granddaughter. It had been easy to forget that, apparently, since she hadn't even come to see Rachel since the day she'd driven her to the first foster home, three weeks after the accident. She'd called the first year on Rachel's birthday, but not a call, a card, or anything else came for the birthdays or Christmases afterwards. And there had been six birthdays and five Christmases, not that Rachel cared or was counting. She'd given up counting a while back when April 18, the date of the accident, and all the days and months afterward had become too hard to think about. What was the point? It didn't change anything about her shitty life.

Not even one of the four social workers she'd had would want to take a call from her. The list of foster mothers and fathers and the one lesbian couple would not be thrilled to hear from her either. And the Harriets would get their number changed immediately if she dared to call them.

Maybe this Zac guy Warty was talking about has a big trunk in his car, Rachel thought. *I could hide in there and get a drive somewhere when he comes with the groceries.* She shook her head and laughed at herself. *With my luck, he probably drives a horse and buggy.*

Rachel headed out to the bushes she'd seen from the upstairs window. There were about six paths fenced off through the thick growth, and as she got closer to them she realized they were raspberry bushes. A big black dog and a shaggy grey dog were sleeping in the sun nearby, and they just slightly raised their heads when she approached. Amelia was kneeling beside the bushes, placing small green cardboard boxes full of berries in a wooden tray. The three people whose heads Rachel had seen from the window were standing there, each holding another full box. Two of them were girls who looked like mirror images of each other, except one was wearing pink shorts and a purple tank top and the other one was wearing purple shorts and a pink tank top. Their identical heads had massive tangles of red curls and they looked like they should

13

break into a chorus of "The Sun Will Come out Tomorrow." The other was a boy who was as wide as he was tall.

"This is Chelsea, Crystal, and Raymond," Amelia said as she passed Rachel an empty box.

Tweedle Dee and Tweedle Dum and Balloon Boy, Rachel thought as she started dropping raspberries into the box Amelia had passed to her, getting the unspoken message that she was to start picking.

"And our lazy dogs are Sam and Bud. Not guard dogs by any means. I just read somewhere yesterday that in a town in Oklahoma you could be sent to jail for making an ugly face at a dog."

Rachel had picked two boxes of raspberries before she heard the call for lunch. Amelia was draining a pot into the white enamel sink when she entered the kitchen. Chelsea was filling glasses with ice water and Crystal was carrying a plate of chicken to the table. Raymond was already sitting down, slathering half a pound of butter onto a roll.

"Rachel, get the pickles from the fridge please," Amelia instructed, turning slightly toward a doorway at the end of the kitchen. "The bowls are on the middle shelf in the pantry. Get one for mustard, one for chow, and another one for the beets."

Again it seemed to Rachel that Amelia was speaking a different language. *What's chow?* she wondered as she walked toward the ancient-looking fridge. The handle on the Frigidaire pulled down stiffly and when the heavy door opened she began her search for something that looked like what she guessed were some kind of pickles.

Amelia came up behind her with a bowl of steaming potatoes in one hand and reached in the fridge with the other, lifting a jar off the shelf. "These mustard pickles are my grandmother's famous recipe. I never thought I could make them as well as she did but after about 30 years of practice I've got it down pat. This is our last bottle of last year's batch. We'll have to get started on this year's supply next week. I asked Zac to get me lots of sugar and white vinegar at the grocery store today. We've got lots of cucumbers in the garden still, though some of them are getting too big. I don't like the great big ones. Speaking of big things, the largest living thing on the earth is a mushroom underground in Oregon that measures 3½ miles in diameter."

Rachel took the bottle from her thinking, *Does this woman ever shut up?* Amelia passed her a larger bottle and then pulled out a third one and carried it across the room and into the pantry, setting the potatoes on the table as she walked by. "This is green tomato chow-chow. We made that last week. We made 15 bottles, but I gave Zac 5 of them. Chow is his favourite and as good a cook as he is he doesn't try to make pickles or jam. I'm happy to do it for him, though. God knows he does enough for us."

The pantry was a small square room with shelves on three sides. The end wall had a wide counter that came out about a metre past the bottom shelf. There was a large wooden board on it that was covered with flour and bit of dough. Beside the board sat a rack with more of the rolls Raymond was eating. *At least there'll be some left for me if Balloon Boy devours the whole basketful on the table by the time I get there,* Rachel thought to herself.

Amelia set three bowls on the counter and opened the jar of chow-chow. Then she walked out of the pantry, grabbed two pots from the stove, drained them into the sink, and put the contents in bowls. She was sitting down by the time Rachel had filled the small bowls with the pickles and carried them to the table.

Everything smelled really good. There were pieces of chicken covered with a light-brown coating, potatoes, peas, and yellow and green beans. There was also a bowl of some sort of orange-coloured lumpy stuff that Rachel didn't recognize. They had been lucky to get any vegetables at all at the Harriets', and if they did they came from a Green Giant bag.

"Pass the squash to Rachel, please, Raymond. Eat up now, kids. You worked hard this morning. 31 boxes. It looks like our raspberry crop will be good this year. Whatever we pick tomorrow we'll either use for jam or put in the freezer for later. We wouldn't want to be caught short for the winter by getting greedy and selling them all. There is nothing like the smell of raspberries on a cold February day to give you the hope of summer."

Rachel filled her plate and even tried the squash, which was something she had never tasted before. She spooned some mustard pickles beside her potatoes but stayed away from the chow and the red round things she assumed were the beets.

Amelia just kept talking though the whole lunch. Rachel wasn't sure how she had time to take a bite of food between sentences. Chelsea and Crystal didn't say a word but seemed interested in the conversation. Raymond laughed at something Amelia said but never stopped chewing long enough to speak. Rachel just ate quietly, consumed by thoughts of how to escape this nuthouse and barely hearing what Amelia was saying.

"I suppose we will have to start peeling the potatoes soon," Amelia said to Rachel, breaking through her thoughts and bringing her back to the conversation. "I love the new ones that we can eat skin and all. We are going to have a good crop this year, I think. Raymond has kept them well hoed up and I haven't found a sunburned one yet. The largest potato grown was in Lebanon. It weighed 24.9lbs. We'll be lucky if a couple of our turkeys weigh that much."

Rachel noticed that Amelia always said we—*we* this, *our* that. Most of what she was saying meant nothing to Rachel, who wasn't going to be a part of this *we*, no matter what Amelia said. She wondered how long the others had been here and if they felt like they were part of the *we*. Mrs. Thompson had said on the drive out that Miss Walton had been taking in children who had nowhere else to go since she had left her job at the New Brunswick Protestant Orphanage in the early 70s. Apparently Social Services had complete faith in her methods and she had done wonders with some *very difficult* children.

Rachel had not missed the emphasis Mrs. Thompson had put on the words *very difficult*. The funny part was that Social Services seemed to have complete faith in the Harriets' methods, too, and Rachel was quite sure if they really knew what some of those methods were, that wouldn't be the case. *Is it a good method to tie an 18-month-old boy to his crib by both legs to keep him from trying to climb out?* Rachel wondered. *Should Bob really buy his cigarettes and beer with the birthday money of a kid too stupid to tell anybody?*

Amelia stood up and took her plate to the sink. Then she walked over to the stove, swung down the door of a long compartment, grabbed a potholder, and pulled out a still-warm pie. The crust was light brown with blotches of deep blue juice that had bubbled in places on the sides and top.

"My grandmother always said it's not a good blueberry pie if it doesn't boil over in the oven. If that's true, then this one is going to be excellent."

Crystal got up and poured the boiling water from the kettle into a brown teapot. Then she grabbed a cup and saucer covered with purple flowers from the pantry and set it down in front of where Amelia had been sitting. Rachel stared at the pie as Amelia started cutting generous pieces, placing them on small glass plates. She had not seen a homemade pie in any of the other places she had lived. Looking at the golden crust, she remembered when she and Caleb would get on stools on either side of their mother and watch her roll pastry out with a rolling pin. She would always let them take a turn rolling and if they messed up she would laugh and patch the crust together. "It doesn't matter what it looks like, it just matters if it tastes good," she would always say.

Chelsea got up, poured the steaming tea into the cup, and passed Amelia a plastic bottle that looked like a beehive. Without a word they both sat back down and started eating their pieces of blueberry pie. *What were they,* wondered Rachel, *the tag team tea girls?*

"A cup of tea on Walton Lake Road," Amelia said to Rachel. "What could beat it, except I suppose high tea at the Empress Hotel? I've always dreamed about having high tea at the Empress Hotel. But these girls are the next best thing. They always make me a lovely cup of tea with just a spoonful of honey—and always in my favourite cup and saucer. Pansies have beautiful expressive faces and I always see sweet faces on the pansies on this beautiful cup. Honey is the only food that does not spoil. Honey has been found in tombs of Egyptian Pharaohs and when tasted by archaeologists they found it to be still edible."

Chapter 2

Wet Dogs and Underwear

Rachel was up to her elbows in hot soapy water. Raymond held a red checked dishcloth and dried each dish she set on the drainer as if it were a treasured family heirloom. After he dried it, he passed it to Crystal, who would walk into the pantry to put it away on the shelf. This laborious exercise, combined with the silence, made the task seem almost dream-like to Rachel. *Maybe this* is *a dream,* she thought to herself. *And soon I'll wake up back in my bedroom at the Harriets' and none of the crap of the last few days will have taken place.* She had long given up hoping a dream would take her back to waking up at 619 Regent Street with her Mom's or Caleb's voice breaking through her sleep. In fact, she had long since forgotten what either of those voices sounded like.

Amelia had gone to lay down for a nap. Before going upstairs, she had explained to Rachel that Chelsea had asked for her hour today right after lunch. The hour thing apparently was one of the two so-called rules that Amelia had. The first was that everyone was required to spend one hour a day alone at the lake. The second was "Do Your Part." Rachel thought both rules sounded really stupid. *An hour alone at the lake. What kind of a rule is that?* Rachel wondered.

Amelia had told Rachel that when Chelsea came up from the lake she could go down for her hour. Apparently they took turns choosing their hours in order of their birthday months. She'd said that tomorrow Rachel would get first choice and then they would continue with their rotation. It didn't seem to Rachel like such a big thing to get first choice of when you could sit by a lake for an hour by yourself.

Rachel was just washing the roasting pan that the chicken had been cooked in when Raymond let out a squeal that sounded sort of like the name Zac. It was the first word that had been said in the kitchen since Amelia had left the room. Raymond threw the dish towel down on the drainer and rushed out the door. Rachel could hear a man's voice holler, "Hey, Buddy!" from the yard and she looked out the window to see a tall skinny man with shoulder-length hair who she assumed was Zac passing a box of groceries to Raymond. *Not much wonder he's so excited,* Rachel thought. *The kid obviously loves food.*

Crystal walked out the door and Chelsea came around the corner of the house at the same time. They both hugged Zac before grabbing boxes of groceries from the back of his truck. Rachel let the lukewarm water out of the sink and rinsed the grime from the sides. If nothing else, Margaret Harriet had taught her how to clean stuff. Rachel wondered who was doing her dirty work now.

Raymond was talking a mile a minute as he told Zac all the exciting news of the day: 31 boxes of raspberries, Sam killed a mole, a chicken got out, and he had seen the loons at the lake this morning.

"You must be Rachel," Zac said as he walked into the kitchen. He extended his arm for a handshake. Rachel wiped her wet hand on her pant leg and clumsily shook Zac's hand. "Amelia said I should get some extra groceries and something as a special treat for you. I bought you some peaches. You haven't tasted heaven until you've had Amelia's peach cobbler smothered with whipped cream. This basket is all yours, though, so you can decide if you want her to use some for a cobbler or if you just want to eat them all yourself.

I got another basket of peaches for everyone else, and a couple of bags of Ketchup chips for you all to share."

He turned toward the other kids, who were looking at him like he was some lanky version of Santa Claus. "Raymond, let's you and I go see where that chicken got out while the girls put the groceries away. Oh, and I picked up the part I ordered for the David Brown. Maybe tomorrow afternoon you could come over and help me take the old fuel filter off and put the new piece on?"

Raymond followed Zac out the door. Rachel picked up the basket of peaches Zac had set on the table in front of her. She couldn't remember the last time she had eaten a fresh peach. She picked one up and felt the fuzzy skin on her fingertips. She set it back in the basket, then picked it up again, not quite able to believe that these were really all for her. She looked down at her peach again, then took a big bite and felt the juice drip down her chin, savouring the sweetness. She turned her head away from the twins, who were walking back and forth from the grocery boxes to the pantry. *I'm almost crying, for God's sake,* she reprimanded herself. *It's just a peach. What's wrong with me?*

Sam and Bud followed Rachel down the hill toward the lake. *Does it count as an hour alone if the dogs are with me?* she wondered. Truthfully, she was really quite pleased that both dogs had followed her and not stayed in the garden where Chelsea and Crystal were picking yellow beans. Raymond and Zac were doing something over at the shed where Rachel guessed the chickens were kept. She could hear the pounding of a hammer. The sound faded as she got closer to the water. Sam dropped a stick at Rachel's feet and she picked it up, assuming that he wanted her to throw it. She flung it a ways out into the water and Sam bounded into the lake after it.

Rachel sat on a nearby rock and untied her laces. Sam had the stick back on the ground in front of her before she'd had time to remove her sneakers and socks. She threw it a bit farther this time. She watched as Bud, who was a little ways down the shore, explored a flower of some kind that was swaying in the breeze. Sam came back and dropped his stick again. This time Rachel waded out into the lake a bit before throwing it. After a few more throws, Sam took the stick in his mouth and curled up in a sunny spot on the shore.

Rachel walked to the end of the dock and sat down, dangling her feet in the cool water. Bud followed her out and sat down on the weathered boards beside her. Rachel stared at the gently rippling water. She wondered if they swam in this lake. The kids at the Harriets' all had memberships to the aquatic centre down the street, but Rachel had always refused to go. She told them there was no way she was going to waste her time there when she could be hanging out with her friends at the ball field or the skate park. But the real reason she never went was because she didn't know how to swim. She couldn't even do the dog paddle. She thought about walking out to her waist and letting herself drop into the water. *What would it feel like to float?* she wondered.

A large fly buzzed around Rachel's head and she swatted it with her hand. Bud moved closer and laid his head on her lap. Rachel patted his head and shifted her weight a bit. She could hear the hammering sound again. She heard another sound she guessed was a bird. She closed her eyes, listening to the echoing call. In the background she could hear the lapping of the water and the trees moving slightly in the breeze. The sound of Bud's breathing was mixed with the other sounds. It was so very quiet here, yet not quiet at all.

Rachel heard Amelia call her name. She stood up and walked to the end of the dock, shaking off the cramp in her leg from sitting too long in one position. Sam raised his head and shook himself awake. He picked up his stick and brought it to Rachel again. She threw it toward the path that led up the hill. Both dogs started the walk up without her as she put her socks and sneakers back on. When she stood up she could see that Amelia was walking down the path toward her.

"Did you hear the loons?" Amelia asked as she got closer. "There's a pair and two young ones on the lake this year. If you're really lucky they will come close enough for you to have a good look at them." Amelia continued talking before Rachel had a chance to answer. "Did Sam keep you busy throwing his stick? You met Zac, did you? He and Raymond have gone for a load of firewood now. He'll bring us the kitchen wood first and after we get that all in the shed he'll bring the furnace wood. We put that in the basement through the end window. Zac has a chute thing rigged up that makes putting it in pretty easy. Then we stack it up against the north wall."

The fact that Rachel didn't say anything didn't keep Amelia from talking the whole way up to the house. They stopped at the end of the house where a clothesline was set up. Colourful clothes filled the line from one end to the other. Amelia picked up a large wicker basket that sat on the ground and passed it to Rachel. "Take the clothes off the line and bring them in, please. I'm going inside to make a chicken pot pie for supper. You can fold the laundry, and then I'll show you where everything goes and give you a tour of the rest of the house."

Rachel pulled the line toward her, none too happy about having to touch what she supposed was everybody's underwear. As if reading her mind, Amelia stopped and turned back toward her. "Can you believe there's a law in the state of Minnesota that makes it illegal to hang male and female underwear on the same clothesline? Silly, isn't it? It's just a piece of clothing like any other." She laughed to herself as she headed into the house.

Two sets of underwear in assorted pastel colours were the first things Rachel took off the line. The days of the week were embroidered on the front of them and both Fridays were missing. *Tweedle Dee and Tweedle Dum take the organizing of their undergarments very seriously*, she thought. Next came several large pairs of boxers. She took the clothespins off them quickly and dropped them in the basket, trying not to think about the big butt they covered. Then there was a row of granny panties. She couldn't believe she was going to have to fold them. Socks came next. About twenty pairs stretched out along the line. Then she took off several T-shirts and blouses. A huge pair of blue jeans came next and as Rachel set them in the basket she laughed, thinking that she could probably get her entire body into one leg of these massive things. Several towels and face cloths were the last things on the line. After taking them off, she put the clothespins in a bag hanging nearby and picked up the laundry basket. As she walked toward the house she could see the twins lying on opposite ends of a hammock fastened to two old trees in the middle of the lawn. They were giggling as Crystal made the hammock sway from side to side. The first word she had heard either of them say came from Chelsea as she hollered for her sister to stop.

The kitchen was very hot when Rachel walked in with the laundry basket. Amelia was putting a piece of wood in the stove while holding the lid in her other hand with a tool of some kind. "I need a hot fire to cook the crust of the pie," she explained, hanging the tool on the back of the stove and walking over to the table.

Rachel could see that there was a dish on the table already filled with chicken and vegetables. Amelia spooned gravy onto the mixture then carried the dish into the pantry. Rachel could hear the sound of the wooden rolling pin clunking against the counter, and a couple of minutes later when Amelia emerged, the pie was covered with pastry. She opened the oven door and slid it onto the rack.

"I may as well stick a peach cobbler in the oven while it's hot," Amelia said as she walked over to the table and reached for a peach from the communal basket. She peeled the skin, cut it away from the pit, and sliced it into a baking dish.

Rachel folded the towels and facecloths and set them on a chair. She picked up a flowered blouse and started to fold it. "The peaches are really good." The sound of her own voice startled Rachel. She couldn't even remember putting the thought together and deciding to speak it—the words had just come out and at first she wasn't even sure if Amelia had heard her.

"Have another one," Amelia answered. "That whole basket is yours and they go bad so quickly. It's like so much else in our lives. We have to enjoy it while we have it."

Amelia pushed Rachel's basket toward her. Rachel noticed that she had left the pit of the first one she ate in the basket. She picked it out and set it on the newspaper that held the peelings and pits of the ones Amelia was putting in the dish and then picked out another peach. She sat down and took a bite. The second peach seemed sweeter and tasted even better to her than the first one had.

Rachel followed Amelia into a room with an old couch and chair. A larger table surrounded by an assortment of wooden chairs sat off to the side. There was a desk in one corner and Rachel could see an old-fashioned black phone sitting on it. *So there* is *communication with the outside world, after all,* Rachel thought.

Amelia led Rachel upstairs. At the top of the stairs was a landing with an old rocking chair and a big trunk sitting near a window. A rug made with squares of bright colours sat on the floor in front of the rocker. Several doors led to rooms off the landing, but they were all closed. Amelia pointed to each of the doors and told Rachel whose bedroom it was without opening them. "We try to keep our privacy here, though I will check your room now and again," she said. "Oh, and in an old house like this is you don't want to leave food lying around or we'll be overrun with mice."

Amelia opened a door and walked into the room. There was no window so she had to pull a chain on a fixture hanging from the ceiling for them to be able to see. Every wall of the room was lined from floor to ceiling with shelves, and each shelf was filled with books or magazines. There were also books piled on the tables, benches, and chairs. One wall was completely filled with yellow-bound *National Geographic* magazines.

"January 1915 is the first *National Geographic* we have. My grandmother said that her father began subscribing to the magazine when she was ten years old. They kept getting it just about every year after that except for a few years during the Second World War. I still get it. It wouldn't seem right to stop now."

Amelia walked over and opened a door on the far wall and Rachel could see that it led into her bedroom.

"You can come through this room from your bedroom to reach the hall and the front staircase. Feel free to read any book you like. They are in no special order except for the *National Geographic*s, which are organized by month and year. I'd better go down and make sure that the crust of my pie isn't burning and finish making the cobbler. Take your time and look over the books if you want, then grab the laundry from downstairs and put it away. You can put the towels in the cupboard in the bathroom downstairs, then bring the basket up here and leave it on the trunk in the hall. We can all put our own clothes away later."

Rachel didn't know where to start. This was probably the most books she had ever seen in one place besides the public library. There hadn't been anything to read at the Harriets' except for a couple of Reader's Digest condensed books. She picked up an armload of books that were stacked on the chair nearest to her and carried them through the door into her bedroom. She couldn't get over the fact that she could walk right into a room next door and pick anything she wanted to read from hundreds of books. Right next door were enough books to fill her craving to read other people's stories so she wouldn't have to think anything about the miserable story of her own life. She sat on the side of the bed for just a minute or two before heading down to get the laundry.

"I was right about the cobbler, wasn't I?" asked Zac as he pulled down the tailgate of his truck. Supper was finished, Raymond had gone to the lake, and Chelsea, Crystal, and Amelia were doing the dishes. Rachel had been told to help Zac unload the firewood.

Zac began to fill his arms with wood. Rachel followed his lead by placing some sticks across her arms and then setting them down on the pile in the woodshed the way he did. Even if she wanted to talk to Zac, it felt like any words she might say were stuck in her throat. She had never had trouble talking before, and as a matter of fact she had constantly been told by Bob to shut her smart mouth. Rachel always pretended that it was a compliment to be told she had a smart mouth even though she knew very well that it wasn't what Bob meant. It seemed to Rachel that the drunker he got, the smarter her mouth got. Sometimes her mouth got so smart that he would try to slap it, though he almost always missed. His aim got worse the more he drank, too.

Rachel would've liked to ask Zac some questions. Where did he live? Did he live by himself? What was wrong with Amelia's face? Why did Chelsea and Crystal not seem to talk to anyone but each other? Where was the school around here? Questions kept coming to her brain, but she never opened her mouth. Instead she just continued to load the wood in her arms, carry it into the shed, and place it on the neat stack, trying not to walk into Zac as he did the same. Zac wasn't asking her any questions either, and she was glad about that. Talking about herself was one thing she definitely hated doing.

It was dark when they finished unloading the wood. Rachel looked toward the house and suddenly it hit her that she was staying here. She would have to sleep in this place and she started to feel a nervousness she hadn't felt all day. It wasn't like she hadn't been dropped in strange places before, and it wasn't anything great sleeping in her old room at the Harriets', but this place was so different. It was so quiet here. There was no sound of traffic, no voices, no police sirens, and no lights to be seen. *How am I going to sleep here?* she wondered.

"I'm going to take the raspberries up to the Farmers' Market in the morning and you can come with me if you want," Zac said as he walked back toward his truck.

He closed the tailgate and turned to face Rachel, who still had not said a word. "I can show you some of the sights of the peninsula. You might want to see where the school is, though if you're anything like I was at your age, the last thing you want to think about right now is going back to school in September. If you want to come, be ready by 7:30."

Zac jumped into the driver's seat of his truck. "Look at those stars," he said, pointing up at the brilliant canvas above them. "You don't see a sky like that in the city." Then he closed the door, put the truck in gear, and drove away.

Rachel stared up at the sky as she walked back toward the veranda. The stars were almost hypnotizing. "Look at the stars!" she remembered Caleb saying when he was little. "There must be a hundred of them!" She and her mom had teased him about that for a long time. Rachel saw a brighter star moving through the sky. She closed her eyes and silently spoke their names before she turned and ran into the house.

Rachel fell asleep quickly. She didn't hear a thing until Amelia knocked on her door in the morning. She got dressed, went through the book room, down the front stairs, and into the bathroom. She washed her face quickly before heading into the kitchen, which smelled of frying bacon. Zac was sitting at the table drinking a cup of coffee.

Amelia served Rachel up a plate of blueberry pancakes. "If you want to help Zac at the market this morning, you can keep a dollar from every box of raspberries you sell," she said as she set the syrup on the table. "The girls bagged some yellow beans yesterday, so they can have the money from those. Raymond gets half the egg money this week. Did you know that a fresh egg will sink but a stale egg floats? Oh, and the lake today, when do you want your hour?"

Zac stood up and set his cup beside the sink. "It's going to be a hot day, Amelia. I'll take the kids swimming later when we get back from the market. Are you ready, Rachel?" He walked out the door without waiting for an answer.

"I'll take my hour after supper," Rachel told Amelia. She rolled the last bite of pancake through the syrup left on her plate, finished it, and hurried to put on her orange sneakers.

Rachel carried the first wooden tray of raspberries to a long table on the veranda of the log building that housed the Kingston Farmers' Market. People were already waiting at the table and one woman reached for a box as Rachel set the tray down.

"I'll take three boxes of raspberries," the woman said. "And two dozen eggs please."

Rachel looked at the coins in the coffee can Zac passed her. She counted the change before she put the woman's money in. Rachel had always kept a bit of the change when Margaret or Bob had sent her to the store. They never seemed to count it and never caught on. But today she was going to keep track of all the money and give every cent back to Amelia. It was too early to take that chance.

The morning went quickly and by about 11:00 everything had been sold. Zac had let Rachel do all the selling and had spent most of his time walking around and talking to people. He had even brought a few people over to the table to meet Rachel, as if she were some celebrity or something. He knew a lot more about her than she thought he did. He knew her last name, her age, and what grade she was going into. One woman said that her daughter was going into Grade 8, too, and that she would tell her to look out for Rachel when school started. Zac also introduced Rachel to a man named Roger and told her he would be her bus driver. He shook her hand and joked about her always being able to get the back seat since Amelia's kids were the first kids on the bus in the morning.

Zac bought a loaf of bread, some doughnuts, and a couple packages of meat before they got in the truck and started for home.

"Why doesn't Wart—I mean, Amelia—come to the market herself?" asked Rachel.

Zac slowed down a bit and turned toward Rachel. "She doesn't leave home," he said.

At first Rachel thought Zac was going to say more, but he didn't. She wanted to ask about Amelia's face. Nobody had said a word about it and Rachel wondered how anyone could ignore it or pretend it looked normal.

"This is Macdonald Consolidated School," Zac said as he pulled into a driveway in front of the school and shut off the truck's engine. "It goes up to Grade 8, so you'll go here for one year, then move on to Hampton High School when you start Grade 9."

Rachel looked out at the big building. "Did you go to this school?" she asked.

"Yes," Zac answered.

"Are you Amelia's son?" Rachel blurted out, realizing she hadn't even considered before that he could be Amelia's son. He didn't call her Mom, though.

"No. I was a foster kid just like you. I ended up at Amelia's when I was eleven years old. Let's get you home. We're just like a Brinks truck sitting here with all the money you made this morning." Zac laughed and pulled out of the schoolyard.

They were turning on to Walton Lake Road when Rachel spoke again. "I don't know how to swim."

"Don't worry about that," Zac said. "I'll teach you."

Rachel passed the coffee can to Amelia as soon as she walked into the kitchen. Amelia stood up, wiped her wet hands on a towel, and set it on top of the fridge.

"I'll get you to count it after you eat lunch. How did it go? I suppose Zac found lots of people to gab with and left all the work to you. He does like to take someone with him so he can make the rounds. We've already eaten. There's some corn on the cob in the pot on the stove, but before you sit down go holler to Zac to come have some, too. We've been cutting up mustard pickles all morning. You can ask Raymond what he was crying about. He chopped the onions. I'm just finishing up the cucumbers and then we'll be done. I'll stop talking and let you go get Zac."

Rachel cleared off the kitchen table and washed the dishes she and Zac had used. Zac had left in a hurry, remembering he had to get home and put the meat he'd bought into the freezer. Amelia had covered the ingredients for the pickles and set them on the counter in the pantry. She was now drinking tea from her pansy cup. The other kids were sitting at the table waiting for their money. Amelia passed the can to Rachel and asked her to count it and divide it up.

Rachel already knew exactly the amount, but carefully counted it out loud, separating the bills and the change right down to the pennies. She began reciting the amounts for each of the things they sold.

"We sold all the raspberries and that was $77.50. We made

$20 from the yellow beans. The eggs sold almost as soon as we got there and that gave us $18.00. That gives us $115.50. There was $5.00 in change to begin with, so the total is $120.50."

Rachel began scooping up the money to put back in the can, but Amelia stopped her, saying, "You can take your money and give the kids what they get. Give Zac $20.00 for gas when he gets back. You may have to hide it in his glove box. He always refuses to take it, but if he finds it later he keeps it. He needs money as much as the rest of us."

Rachel kind of liked the sound of being included in that *us*. She also liked how it felt to be trusted. Being trusted was not something she was used to. She counted out the $9.00 for Raymond and passed it to him. She gave the twins each $10.00. She set aside a $20 bill for Zac and then counted out $31.00 for herself. She put the rest of the money back in the can and passed it across the table to Amelia.

"I don't deserve the $31.00," Rachel said. "I only picked two boxes yesterday." She held out the money in her hand.

"But you did your part," Amelia answered. "That's what we do around here. And when we all do our part, we all share in the rewards. Now why don't you take your money upstairs and get your bathing suit on? Zac will be back in a couple of minutes and it's a perfect afternoon for a swim. I'm going to pick some raspberries while you all go to the lake. You can help me when you come back up, if you like."

Amelia grabbed a straw hat off a peg by the back door and headed outside.

When Rachel got to the lake, the dogs, the kids, and Zac were already in the water. She'd put shorts and a T-shirt on, as the only bathing suit in her stuff was way too small. She couldn't even remember for sure if it had been hers. It might have belonged to one of the other kids at the Harriets' and been put in her dresser by mistake. Raymond was wearing shorts and a huge T-shirt that was literally ballooning out around him as he waded out past his waist. The twins were already swimming and Rachel was pretty sure they would be wearing matching bathing suits.

Zac saw Rachel walking down the path and walked up to meet her. "The first thing you need to do is get wet. All I want you to try to do today is get your face wet. You decide how you want to do that. If you don't mind getting your face wet you can learn to swim underwater. When you can do that, the rest comes easier."

Sam ran toward her and dropped his stick. He shook his wet body and Rachel laughed as she felt the water drops hitting her.

"I may as well just run right in," she said as she kicked off her sneakers. "I'm already wet!"

Rachel sat on the dock after supper for her hour alone. She looked at the glasslike water and thought back to this afternoon. Zac had said she'd done really well for the first day. She hadn't minded getting her face wet, and by the end of the afternoon she was letting herself lie facedown in water that was up past her knees. She hadn't floated exactly, but she had let herself go more and more.

After swimming, Rachel had picked ten boxes of raspberries and Amelia had put most of them in the freezer for the winter. Rachel had eaten a bowl of berries with milk and sugar for dessert and she could still almost taste the sweetness. She'd grabbed the last two peaches from her basket to eat at the lake. As she finished them, she pitched the pits out into the water as far as she could throw them. Neither of the dogs had come with her. Bud had been in the house when she left and Sam had been chewing on a hambone in the front yard.

It was different being here at this time of the day. Everything seemed calmer and more peaceful. It seemed like a long time had passed since she was at the market this morning. She had stashed her money in the pocket of her winter coat and stuck it at the very back of the closet. She didn't think the other kids would steal it, but you could never be sure. She really had no clue what they were like or what they would do. Chelsea and Crystal still hadn't said one word to her. Raymond had grunted a few words but he generally didn't acknowledge that she was even around. He talked nonstop to Zac, though. He was over the moon to be going up to Zac's to work on the David Brown, which Rachel now knew was a tractor.

At least she had seen the school she would be going to. Before seeing it, Rachel had pictured a one-room schoolhouse with an outhouse. But it was a big, normal-looking school and maybe it wouldn't be so bad. It did feel like a different century here, though. She wasn't sure if they had the internet here and she hadn't even seen a computer. Normally she would be freaking if she hadn't gone on Facebook in a couple of days, but she hadn't really even missed it for some reason.

Two loons flapped loudly as they rose out of the still water and took flight. Rachel stood on the dock and watched them until they disappeared out of her sight.

Chapter 3

Turkey Feet, Fireflies, and The Last Swim of Summer

The sound of the rain hitting the tin roof woke Rachel up on Sunday morning. She shifted in bed to look out the window. It was raining really hard and the sky was dark. She had no idea what time it was, but she couldn't hear any sounds coming from the kitchen below. She got up quickly and headed down the back stairs to the kitchen. She saw Amelia in the pantry as she passed by, but didn't say anything as she headed toward the washroom. As she passed through the dining room, Rachel could see that the large table was set with seven places. The dishes were white with red roses around the edges. There were birthday napkins at each place.

Amelia was setting two cake pans into the oven when Rachel re-entered the kitchen. A box of cereal, a carton of milk, a bowl, and a spoon were on the table.

"Top of the morning to you, Rachel. I don't cook breakfast on Sunday mornings, so help yourself to cereal or make yourself some toast. On Sundays we get up whenever we want to and

I put all my cooking energy into supper, though I will have to cook up and bottle those pickles today. Did you see our fancy table? We're going to celebrate your birthday since you weren't here in July. Zac and his friend Roger are coming for supper. Did you know that the proper response to the Irish greeting "Top of the Morning to You" is "And the Rest of the day to Yourself"?

Even with the steady rain, the hour at the lake rotation was still discussed when everyone gathered in the kitchen at around ten o'clock.

"Raymond's birthday is in January, almost a New Year's baby if he had come a few hours earlier," Amelia explained to Rachel as she went through the birthday months that determined the order of choosing time at the lake. "Crystal and Chelsea were born on March 29, with Crystal making her entrance two minutes before Chelsea. You were born in July and my birthday is in November. So we start with Raymond and go in that order for five days and then start over."

"I'm going to take my hour right now," Raymond said as he grabbed a raincoat that was hanging by the back door. "Zac's going to start teaching me to drive the David Brown this afternoon," he hollered, shutting the door behind him.

Rachel got the fourth choice and chose the hour right after Raymond's. She went back upstairs and lay on her bed to read and wait for her turn. Later she heard Zac's voice in the kitchen below and headed back downstairs thinking an hour must have almost passed. She looked out the window on the landing and could see that the rain had stopped and the sky looked a bit brighter.

As she entered the kitchen, she saw that Amelia had just finished frosting the layer cake at the kitchen table. Zac was licking the frosting from one of the beaters and offered the other one to Rachel. The sweet white frosting was still warm and it tasted wonderful. Rachel turned the beater slowly, taking her time to get every last bit of frosting, before setting it in the dishpan. Then she put on her sneakers and headed out the door.

The wood of the dock was dark and wet, but Rachel sat down anyway. She kept her feet propped up on a large rock near the part of the dock that wasn't out in the water. Sam and Bud had followed her down today. Sam got wet chasing his stick into the water, and then settled himself close enough to Rachel to soak her pant leg. Bud jumped up on her, leaving his muddy footprints on her other leg. Rachel just watched the choppy water as each wave rippled into the shore. The warm damp air made her feel a bit drowsy.

When Rachel got back up to the house, there was a small red car in the yard. Bud and Sam sniffed it a bit and Bud let out a quick bark as if to cover himself if confronted with the fact that he was supposed to be a guard dog. He settled himself on the veranda and watched without interest as Rachel entered the house.

When she walked into the kitchen, Rachel saw a young woman sitting at the table.

"Rachel, this is Jodie," Amelia said. "She brought us lunch. Grab a plate and help yourself. There's another pizza in the warming oven so don't worry about taking the last piece in this box."

"Nice to meet you, Rachel," Jodie said. Rachel sat down and began eating a piece of pizza. "Remember when I first got here, Amelia?" Jodie continued. "You had your hands full that winter. Between me, Travis, Jason, and Emily, we sure kept you busy."

"You and Jason got to be good friends that winter, once you decided not to kill each other."

"Oh yeah, I remember the fights we had when I first got here. Remember the time you caught us in the chicken shed throwing eggs at each other?"

"Jason called on Wednesday night. Megan is expecting again in May. Can you believe Logan is going to be three on his birthday?"

Rachel got up for a second piece of pizza, relieved that Amelia and Jodie were talking about stuff that didn't have anything to do with her and that Jodie wasn't asking her questions. She had no intention of telling this person anything about herself.

"You can stay for supper, can't you, Jodie?" Amelia asked. "We're celebrating Rachel's birthday tonight."

"I'll stay if you let me help with dinner," Jodie replied. "Do your part, right? I hear that in my head almost every day. But what better mantra could a person have than that? I wish some of the lazy people at work had been taught it."

"Oh, and Zac and Roger are coming, too, so you'll have a chance to catch up with them as well."

"That's great. I always love to see Zac. When I was your age, Rachel, I had a huge crush on him."

Rachel was not allowed near the kitchen while the others were getting supper ready, so she went into the chicken shed and collected the eggs. One of the eggs was still warm and she rolled it around in her hand, feeling its smooth shell. She set the basket of eggs on the veranda and then walked out to the end of the driveway. Zac and Raymond were there. Zac was walking beside Raymond as he drove the big white tractor slowly along the road.

Zac saw Rachel standing at the end of the driveway and motioned for her to catch up. "Put it in third gear, Raymond."

The tractor sped up a bit and Rachel ran to meet Zac. They walked a little ways before either one spoke.

"You live in that house with the green roof, don't you?" Rachel asked.

"Yeah," Zac replied. "Do you want to walk down with me and get the truck? I drove the tractor up to give Raymond his lesson. He's a natural. Once he got the hang of the clutch he did just fine. By the time we get to the house, get the truck, and come back, it will almost be time for your birthday supper."

"That girl Jodie is staying for supper. Did you live here when she did?"

"No, I was already gone when she came. I went out west to work for a couple of years and when I got back Jodie had been here for a year I think. She stayed until she graduated from high school four years ago."

"What about the twins and Raymond? How long have they been here?"

"Chelsea and Crystal have been with Amelia since they were five years old, so four years. Raymond came two years ago. Travis just left in June. He was on Hampton High's five-year plan, but he finally graduated from high school. Social Services only pay until kids age out at 18, unless they are still in high school, but Amelia has been known to keep them long after that."

Rachel could see Raymond turning the tractor onto Zac's driveway.

"I never did graduate, but Amelia kept me long after social services cut me loose. She helped me buy this land, too. It belonged to an uncle of hers and when he decided to sell it she got Terry Fullerton to lumber her land for three winters so she could lend me the money to be able to buy it."

By the time they were halfway up the driveway, Rachel could get a good look at the house she had only seen the roof of from the road. It was two storeys high and shaped like a barn. It looked like a stone house, but as she got closer she could she that what she thought were stones were actually the round ends of wood. There were several other buildings around it and she could see some sheep in a fenced-in field over by where Raymond was getting down off of the tractor.

"This is my little piece of paradise," said Zac. It took me about five years to build the house and it is far from finished, but it's all mine. It's nothing fancy, but it's more than I ever dreamed of owning."

"Do you have a job?" Rachel asked, realizing as soon as she said it that it wasn't any of her business.

"I make my living doing a bit of mechanical work for people, cutting and selling firewood, and keeping a few animals," Zac answered.

Rachel looked ahead to see Raymond making his way toward them. His wide smile looked like it might swallow his face.

"You did great, Buddy!" Zac exclaimed. "I'll have you driving for me in the woods in no time. We'll have to teach Rachel to drive sometime, too. Once you can drive that old David Brown, you can drive anything." He nodded toward the sheep pen. "Let's throw a bale of hay in to the sheep, and then we'll head back up the road for supper."

"If a native Hawaiian woman places a flower behind her right ear, it means she is available," Amelia told Jodie. "The bigger the flower, the more desperate she is." She laughed as she handed Jodie the sunflower from the vase of flowers that she had just set in the middle of the table. She turned to see Rachel, Zac, and Raymond coming through the door.

"You guys are just in time. Supper is ready. Roger's been here for a few minutes. The girls have kept him busy trying to catch one of the new kittens in the barn. Raymond, give them a holler to come in. Let's get the birthday girl seated. I'll get the food on the table."

The roast beef dinner was delicious. Rachel drenched her vegetables with rich brown gravy and heaped mustard pickles beside her meat. Every bite was wonderful.

Zac, Jodie, Roger, and Amelia had a great time reliving old memories over dinner. "Remember when I had to use my own money to buy a sheet of gyprock when Matthew Comeau and I kicked a hole in the bathroom wall at school?" Zac said.

"Oh, I remember," answered Amelia. "I remember you asked the principal if you could have the rest of the sheet because the janitor only used part of it to fix the hole."

"He brought it home on the bus," Roger added.

"I gyprocked one wall of my tree house with it," Zac laughed. "I was getting my money's worth."

After dinner, Jodie and the twins cleared off the table while Amelia served the tea and coffee. When everyone was seated again, Amelia got up and brought out the cake, setting it down in front of Rachel. Zac stood up and lit the thirteen candles that were sticking out from the wavy white frosting.

In July, for Rachel's real birthday, Margaret had bought a cake at the Superstore that was three days past its best-before date, and the memory of the sawdusty taste put a lump in her throat. In her head she could hear Bob's loud voice singing an off-key rendition of "Happy Birthday." He had followed up his singing with an unsuccessful attempt to give her a pinch to grow an inch and then he had almost fallen flat on his drunken ass.

Rachel blew out the candles, cut the first piece, and passed it to Zac. She didn't bother making a wish, though. *What's the point of making wishes when what you most wish for could never come true?* she thought to herself.

The next week went quickly, each day filled with lots of chores. On Monday morning Rachel and Amelia had to cut up another batch of mustard pickles. On Tuesday Amelia got Rachel to cook them, watching while she stood over the hot stove, stirring the heavy bubbling pot so the contents wouldn't burn. Rachel had poured the thick yellow mixture into the bottles all by herself, and she had actually felt pretty proud when she'd finally tightened the hot lids to seal them. On Wednesday afternoon Rachel had helped everyone fill the shed with the rest of the kitchen wood. On Thursday, when Zac came to bushwhack part of the lower field, he got Rachel to drive the tractor. She'd stalled it a couple of times, but he'd gotten her to try again. She had gotten it into second gear and stopped it without hitting anything. On Friday they picked squash, dug potatoes, and pulled some carrots, putting them in bags for the market. On Saturday, while the twins were at the market with Zac, Rachel, Amelia, and Raymond had spent the morning cleaning the basement so that there was room to put the furnace wood in. Rachel had also helped Amelia roll out and bake molasses cookies. The egg money this week had been Rachel's and she'd added that money to what she got last week.

It was now Sunday morning and Rachel was sitting on the dock. It had been early when she'd come downstairs to the dark kitchen and no one else was up. She'd grabbed a couple of cookies from the jar in the pantry before heading down to the lake. The sun was just rising in the sky as she walked down the path toward the water.

Rachel had spent a lot of time at the lake over the last few days. They had gone swimming every day and even Amelia had gotten in the water on Wednesday. Rachel was swimming underwater with no trouble now and she was also getting better at staying afloat in deeper water. Zac said he bet she would be jumping off the raft before they had to haul it in for the winter.

Last night, Rachel's hour alone at the lake was at dusk and she hadn't wanted to come up when Amelia had called her in. It would have been amazing to curl up in a sleeping bag on the shore and stay in this beautiful place all night. The way she felt at the lake was not something she could put words to. She could think here, and it didn't matter if she thought about things that made her want to cry, because there was no one here that she had to hide from. Last night she had cried and Sam and Bud had looked at her with their big eyes and squeezed up to her on either side. She still couldn't believe she had actually let herself cry.

Right after the accident, Rachel had cried. Mrs. Clark, their next-door neighbour, had been the one to tell Rachel that her mom and brother were both dead. Rachel had been sitting on the front step, waiting for them to get home. She could clearly remember seeing Mrs. Clark walking across the yard. She was walking in slow motion and the look on her face was not like anything Rachel had ever seen before. Not in real life, anyway. Rachel knew before Mrs. Clark even spoke that it was her Mom and Caleb. Somehow she knew just by the look on Mrs. Clark's face and the way she walked that what she was about to say was going to be the worst thing in the world.

Mrs. Clark had hugged her tightly and said, "Cry, honey. Go ahead and cry." But during the next few days, Rachel had quickly realized that crying was not going to change anything or take the pain away, and she hadn't cried since.

Rachel walked along the shore to the place where the brook ran into the lake. She sat on a large rock nearby and threw Sam's stick for him. She could hear the loons crying in the still morning air.

"In Alabama it is illegal to play dominoes on Sunday," Amelia said as she set the box of dominoes on the table. Supper was over and Zac was helping Rachel put the dishes away. Raymond had washed and the twins had dried. Rachel was glad for the chance to move around. The second piece of apple pie piled high with butterscotch ripple ice cream had left her feeling a bit uncomfortable.

"If I didn't eat all week, Sunday supper at Amelia's would do me." Zac laughed as he set a stack of plates on the pantry shelf. "Sunday night supper and a good game of turkey foot dominoes. That is always a good way to start a new week."

"Hurry up," called Amelia from the other room. "Rachel has been here over a week and we haven't even taught her how to play dominoes yet."

After a few rounds, Rachel was starting to catch on to the game. She had gotten caught on the second round with the double nothing so her score was the highest, but in the last round she had caught everyone with lots of dominoes, so the scores were getting closer.

When the game was finished the twins carefully placed the dominoes back in the box. Zac had won by 20 points and was doing a little victory dance. "The last Sunday night of summer holidays calls for a bonfire," he announced. "Grab the stuff for s'mores out of the pantry, Raymond," he said as he stood up and put his sweater on. "Are you coming down with us, Amelia?"

"You kids go and have fun," she answered. "I think I'll stay up here. Let me rest my old bones and take a little time to get my wits about me. Tomorrow night we'll be busy getting ready for school. I can't believe how fast the summer went."

The twins jumped up, grabbed their matching fleece hoodies, and headed out the door.

"Did you know that naturalists use marshmallows to lure alligators out of the swamp?" Amelia asked as she passed Rachel an orange flashlight. "It's a good thing there are no alligators in Walton Lake." She stood at the screen door, able to feel the summer breeze, and listened as the kids' voices faded into the night.

Four kids in school again, Amelia thought to herself with a sigh as she closed the door. She much preferred the summer months, when no outside contact was required of her or of the kids if they didn't want it. The busy summer days of working in the garden and around the farm were good medicine. The beautiful afternoons at the lake were treasures that seemed to bring out the best in them all.

The twins had a hard time at school since they kept so much to themselves. They were both smart as whips and had no trouble with the work, but the social part was difficult for them. Amelia fought the battle every year to convince the principal that they still needed to be in the same class if they were to do well. A whole day separated from each other was more than they could do now and possibly ever. The first few years of their lives had cemented the strong need to protect and shelter each other and that was not something that could easily be set aside.

Raymond took a lot of teasing and bullying from the other kids because of his size. Even though he had shed at least 40 pounds in the last year, he was still much bigger than all of the other kids his age. He was so content here, and he hung off every positive word that Zac gave him. His confidence had grown in leaps and bounds over the summer months and she dreaded his transition back to school.

Amelia didn't know exactly what to expect from Rachel, but her experience told her that there were sure to be some challenges coming. She would make some calls right away and try to get the teachers and the guidance counselor on her side, which she hoped would help with Rachel's settling in.

Zac pulled a log up close to the flames of the bonfire and sat down. Raymond passed Rachel a stick and she stuck a marshmallow onto the end of it. She could hear the twins' excited voices as they ran back and forth along the shore trying to trap fireflies in mason jars. Raymond was rattling on about something to Zac. Rachel stared at her marshmallow as she held it above the flames.

Every summer Rachel's mom had taken her and Caleb camping for a week. For seven days, Rachel and Caleb would run all day long from the beach to the playground and their mom would follow behind them, slathering them with sunscreen and bug spray. Every night they would build a fire in the fire pit at their campsite. Caleb would always fall asleep curled up in their mom's lap with his hands and mouth sticky after eating his fill of roasted marshmallows. Rachel would keep cooking her famous gooey-on-the-inside, perfectly browned, not-burnt-on-the-outside masterpieces and share them with her mom. After a while her mom would carry Caleb into the tent and come back out. Then the two of them would stay in front of the fire until the last ember faded. As it got colder, they would snuggle together on the lounge chair with Rachel's Care Bear sleeping bag wrapped around them both.

Rachel stuck her marshmallow closer to the red coals, turning the stick slowly to brown all sides. She studied its perfection and then stuck it back in the flames, watching it catch fire and melt until the last bit of marshmallow was completely burnt off the stick. Then she stood up, threw the branch into the flames, and left the bonfire. *These people are not my family and that shack is not my home,* Rachel thought as she climbed the hill.

Rachel had been lying awake staring through the window at the moon for a long time. She wished that the summer was just starting. Since getting here she had thought many times about ways she could escape, where she might go, and how trapped she felt being stuck in this forsaken place. But when she really thought about her choices, she had to admit that if the choice was between staying here or going to school, her choice would definitely be to stay here. She knew as she was thinking these thoughts that there was no way she could do that. School was something no one would let her hide from. She would put her tough face on during the day and get by just as she had for the last five years.

Rachel rolled over, pulled up the blankets, and closed her eyes tightly in an attempt to conjure sleep. As a little girl, when she woke up in the night she would quietly tiptoe into her mother's room and crawl into bed beside her. Some nights Caleb would already be there and her mom would move him over and make room for her. Once she snuggled beside her mother she could always go back to sleep, no matter what had woken her. Her mom always pretended in the morning that she was surprised to find them there. Then they would play a game they'd named "Lump," where her mom would start to make the bed while she and Caleb hid under the covers. Her mom would smooth out the blankets and pretend she didn't know what the lumps were as Rachel and Caleb giggled hysterically.

Rachel pulled the covers completely over her head. She squeezed her eyes shut, trying to imagine the feeling of her mom's hands pressing on her as she made the bed. Rachel wished more than anything that the covers would be pulled back suddenly and she would see her mom standing there, laughing.

Rachel watched each orange foot take deliberate steps as she left the bus and began the walk up the long driveway. All she wanted to do was get to her bedroom. All day she had thought of getting back to her room, where she could forget the way being in this new school surrounded by new people had made her feel. At least at her old school she had a routine and a group of kids that didn't have any expectations of her. She had well established the reputation that made people leave her alone. Getting close to her was off-limits and she had worked hard at keeping it that way.

Raymond came up behind Rachel, falling into step with her. He walked along beside her for a couple of minutes before speaking.

"Who's your homeroom teacher?"

"What?" Rachel replied like the words he had spoken were not even English.

"I'm in the 7/8 split. It would have been funny if we had got in the same homeroom."

"Yeah, friggin' hilarious."

Rachel thought back to the morning when she'd stepped off the bus and walked up the stairs into the school. Some gushy woman who she later found out was the TA in her classroom had offered to take her to the office to see what class she was in. The secretary had recognized Rachel from the market and told the TA to take her to Mr. Johnston's room. The TA had chatted the whole way to the room, asking Rachel all kinds of questions and telling her details about the school as if she were some kind of tour guide. Rachel hadn't answered any of them and had showed her enthusiasm for this new school by slamming her locker door before entering her homeroom, which was full of strange kids who stared at her like she had arrived from another planet.

All day long smiling people had asked her stuff. "Where do you live?" "What school did you come from?" "What are your parents' names?" The gym teacher had asked every kid he didn't recognize who their parents were and who their brothers and sisters were, showing great pleasure when he knew the parents or had taught a sibling. Rachel had told him that she was new and that she was in foster care and he'd quickly moved on to the next kid. The whole day had been like that. And then there had been that look—the one the Science teacher had given her when she'd glanced up from her class list and said, "Oh, you're at Amelia Walton's." That one fact had apparently told her all she needed to know about this new kid and the trouble she was likely to make.

Rachel didn't say a word to Amelia as she walked into the kitchen after slamming the screen door. She just hurried past, ignoring her greeting.

"Did you know that carrots are better for us after they are cut with a knife?" Amelia said as Rachel headed for the back stairs. "The slash of the knife kicks up the juice and the carrot pumps out phytochemicals that makes it more nutritious."

"I would love to take a knife to something—or someone—but it wouldn't be a carrot," Rachel muttered as she stomped up the stairs. Rachel could feel tears pricking her eyes by the time she got to the top of the stairs. That just made her even angrier.

Amelia had kept herself busy all day, trying hard not to worry about the kids and what they were facing on this first day of school. She was pleased that Raymond hadn't refused to get on the bus this morning. There had been many days over the last two years when she and Roger and sometimes Zac had needed to force him up the bus steps and into the front seat. Then arriving at the school it sometimes took both the principal and the vice-principal to get him off the bus. The twins had never put up any physical resistance to going to school, but they definitely would show their anxiety in the way they acted, getting extra quiet and even more reclusive. And she hadn't known at all what to expect from Rachel, who had left this morning in a robotic manner, showing nothing at all about how she may be feeling about starting at a new school. The sound of her feet stomping up the stairs a few minutes ago had been the first real emotional reaction Amelia had seen from Rachel since she'd arrived at Walton Lake.

Rachel didn't intend to ever come out of her room. She knew of course that she would have to, but for now she told herself that she was never going to leave. She pictured how she could live her whole life in this room. Amelia and the others would bring her food, and set up a place for her to use the bathroom and wash. They would bring her books and maybe even some kind of work for her to do. She could invite certain people in to visit her, though the list would probably be really short. In fact, she couldn't think of a single person she'd want to put on that list. She lay there, creating her new life, not wanting to think about how horrible her day at school had been. She ignored the call to supper when she heard it. Sooner or later the others would realize that she wasn't leaving this room and they would bring up some food.

She was getting hungry. She hadn't eaten much lunch. She had spent the lunch break sitting alone in the cafeteria, imagining that most of the loud chatter and laughter was from kids talking and laughing about her.

Rachel must have drifted off to sleep because it was almost dark when she heard the knock. The door opened a crack. "You haven't been to the lake today," Amelia said matter-of-factly. "Why don't you get up and go now? There's a plate of food for you in the warming oven. Zac was here with a wagonload of furnace wood and we left you some to put in the basement. You can eat before you go to the lake and I'll help you put the last bit of wood in when you get back up. Zac and the kids are in the middle of a riveting game of dominoes."

Rachel didn't answer Amelia, but she got off her bed and walked downstairs, for now forgetting her plan to stay in her room forever.

The lake this afternoon was more beautiful than Rachel had ever seen it. The water was a gorgeous sapphire blue. The clouds above were white and fluffy, and one of the largest ones looked like a castle with two turrets. Rachel threw Sam's stick and he raced into the water as if the treasure he was after was an unbelievable gift. She laughed at his expectant face when he dropped the stick at her feet again.

She remembered a few nights ago, after the first day of school, when she had come down here just as it was getting dark. Sam and Bud had both come with her, but they didn't bother her for attention. Instead they had just laid down at the edge of the beach as if they were there to guard her. She had thought at the time how foolish she had been to imagine staying in her room forever. If she'd stayed in her room she wouldn't have been able to feel the breeze off the water, see the moonlight stretch across the lake, or hear the waves as they gently hit the shore.

After coming up from the lake, she and Amelia had put the last bit of furnace wood into the basement. The whole time Rachel had kept telling herself that she would be fine. Whatever going to school every day took from her, she would get it back when she obeyed the two rules of staying here: "spend an hour at the lake" and "do your part."

Rachel went for her last swim of the year on a day in late September. Zac and Raymond had just pulled the raft in for the winter that morning. Rachel was really able to swim now, and she swam out to where the water was over her head, then back in to a place where her hands touched the ground, then turned around and did it over again and again. The other kids had left the water a while ago. Chelsea had barely gotten wet, telling Rachel it was too cold. It was the first time she had ever even uttered a word while looking in Rachel's direction, and it had caught Rachel a little off-guard.

Rachel felt like she needed to store every bit of this last swim so it would hold her over the winter. She was worried about missing the feeling she got when she swam, the feeling of being exactly where she wanted to be as she gave herself up to the buoyancy of the water. She let the water hold her now, let it surround her, carry her to a place where she was everything she wanted to be. She would keep this feeling and remember it as the lake changed with the seasons, until the warm weather would give it back to her.

Chapter 4

Snowstorms, Sir Issac Newton, and Family Trees

It began as a singsong murmur that Rachel could hardly hear from her seat at the back of the bus: "Fatty, fatty, two by four." As the bus rounded the corner past the ferry, the chorus became louder and then Raymond was out of his seat, swinging his book bag at the heads of some kids sitting a few seats behind him. Roger brought the bus to a stop, but Raymond continued his attack, swearing and flailing. Roger got up out of his seat and calmly grabbed the book bag, took Raymond's arm, and led him to the front of the bus. The two kids sitting in the front seat quickly moved and Rachel could see Raymond slumped down, covering his face with his arms. Roger got back in the driver's seat and continued on down the road as if nothing had happened.

When Roger pulled the bus into the driveway, the twins were the first ones out. Rachel held back, picking up some of the garbage at the back of the bus while Roger gave Raymond a bus slip and assured him that the kids who were teasing him would be getting one, too. Rachel could see that Raymond had started to cry. Roger left the bus and walked with Raymond to the house. Rachel entered the kitchen right behind them and listened while Roger explained what had happened to Amelia. Raymond went to his room without saying a word.

After Roger left, Amelia went into the pantry and made a peanut butter and banana sandwich. She put it on a tray along with a freshly baked molasses cookie. Then she walked to the fridge, poured a glass of chocolate milk, and added it to the tray.

"They tease him because he is so fat," Rachel spat at Amelia as she started peeling the potatoes for supper. "Maybe if you didn't feed him all the time he would lose weight and it would be easier for him. You're supposed to make things better for him, not make his problems worse!" Rachel's anger took her by surprise—she was almost shaking with rage.

Amelia put the tray down on the kitchen table and gave Rachel a long steady look before speaking.

"Raymond has used food all his life to fill up a place that no amount of food will ever begin to fill. He came to me two years ago, abused and neglected, at a weight that was in danger of ending his life. Little by little, I have tried to fill those empty hurting places with a feeling of belonging and value. I will not take the pleasure of food away from him, but I will try to give him the things he needs to fill up the *holes in his soul*." Amelia picked up the tray and left the room.

Holes in his soul, thought Rachel. *What would it take to fill the holes in mine?* She finished peeling the potatoes, guiding each movement of the paring knife through the blur of her tear-filled eyes.

A light snow covered the ground and flurries were falling as Rachel walked up the driveway on a day in late November. All day Rachel had dreaded coming home. She had been so angry this morning and a bad feeling had sat in the pit of her stomach all day like a heavy rock. As she rounded the turn and walked into the yard, she could see Mrs. Thompson's purple PT Cruiser parked in the driveway. *Amelia probably called her to come and get me*, Rachel thought.

"You are not my mother, *Warty!*" were the words she had screamed at Amelia this morning. She had followed that with "You're just a disgusting wart-covered old woman!" She had just caught the look on Amelia's face as she'd slammed the door behind her. The hurt she saw in Amelia's eyes had haunted Rachel all day.

I don't blame her if she gets rid of me, Rachel thought as she threw her book bag on the veranda, called to the dogs, and headed down to the lake.

Rachel threw Sam's stick along the shore and walked as far as she could away from the dock. Even though it was freezing cold outside and her toes were starting to turn to icicles, she was determined to stay at the lake for her whole hour. It was a rule and she was going to follow it.

When Rachel came up from her hour at the lake, she saw Mrs. Thompson walking to her car. Mrs. Thompson noticed her and beckoned her over. "Amelia said things are going quite well," she said as Rachel reached the car. "If you keep having trouble in Math, Social Services will provide some tutoring money. And Amelia said you haven't used your clothing allowance yet—I can come and take you to the city sometime if you want to get some new clothes."

Rachel nodded, confused, thinking, *Isn't she here to take me away?* But Mrs. Thompson just finished her spiel, gave Rachel a half-hearted hug, and got in her car.

As she watched the PT Cruiser pull away, Rachel let out a huge sigh of relief. She couldn't believe that Mrs. Thompson hadn't come to take her to another foster home. It didn't even seem as if she knew about what happened this morning.

Rachel watched the purple car until it turned off the drive-way, then picked up her book bag and entered the house.

Amelia was shoveling a walkway to the chicken shed. The snow was heavy and each time she lifted the shovel she was reminded of her age—fifty-five—not old, really, but she definitely wasn't as young as she used to be. Her aching muscles were telling her that loud and clear. This was her thirty-first winter here, and even though she always tried to keep herself in the present and be grateful for the life she had, sometimes it hit her hard that she had been exiled to this place. Almost her entire life had been spent running this farm and caring for other people's children. She had always tried to convince herself that she had chosen this life, and it wasn't the horror of her face that had driven her to hide herself away. She rarely let herself have any thoughts of how different her life could have been.

As Amelia turned to dump the shovel, she saw Rachel walking toward her. "The greatest snowfall officially reported in Phoenix, Arizona, was one inch," she said, happy to have her thoughts interrupted. "The first time they got that much snow was on January 20, 1933, and then another inch fell again four years later on the same date."

"That wouldn't be much to shovel, would it?" Rachel replied.

"Would you finish the path, please?" Amelia asked her. "I'm going to head into the house and start making a stew for our supper."

Rachel lost herself in thought as she watched Amelia walk away. Amelia had never once mentioned the rude outburst she'd had two weeks ago or punished her in any way. But the look in Amelia's eyes had stayed with Rachel and made her think more about how her mean thoughts and words had hurt this woman, who'd never done anything to hurt her. She would not call Amelia that awful nickname again.

Rachel sat in math class, willing the day to end. Her class had been taught by supply teachers for the last two days while her regular teacher, Mrs. White, was off with a sprained ankle. And today a new woman was standing at the front of the room. Rachel was already having enough trouble in math, and having three different teachers definitely wasn't helping.

"Do review questions 1, 2 5, 8, and 10 on page 157," the teacher said, wrapping up the lesson. "Your test will be to-morrow."

Rachel opened her notebook and slowly wrote the date and page number, trying to use up as much time as she could. She had no idea how to do any of the questions she'd been assigned. She probably would have asked Mrs. White for help, but she had no intention of letting this stranger know she didn't have a clue how to do any of the questions.

Rachel looked up at the clock and saw that there were only a few more minutes of class left. She put her head back down to the page, returning to the intricate doodling of a meaningless picture.

"Rachel, what question are you on?" asked a voice from above.

Rachel looked up from her book and saw that the supply teacher was standing right behind her, looking at the doodles in her notebook.

"I don't understand this stuff," Rachel mumbled, hoping the bell would ring and save her.

"If you were having trouble, you should have told me," the teacher said, looking at her watch. "I don't have time to help you now. I suggest you get your mom or dad to help you tonight."

Rachel did not respond.

The bell rang and everyone started moving. Rachel picked up her books and rushed from the room. As she walked through the doorway, another kid walked in and Rachel bumped right into him.

"Get out of my way, asshole!" she screamed, pushing him with her free hand.

A few minutes later, Amelia received a call from Mr. Harrison, Rachel's principal, informing her that Rachel had assaulted a fellow student and would be required to do an after-school detention.

"I was unaware of Rachel's anger issues, Miss Walton," Mr. Harrison said in what came through as a slightly accusatory tone. "I am very disappointed that you and Rachel's social worker didn't provide me with that information. I've always tried my best to accommodate your foster children, have I not?"

"Yes, Mr. Harrison," Amelia answered, knowing that a long debate about the shortcomings of the school and how complicated it was knowing what these kids need would take more energy than she had and a lot more time, she was sure, than the principal had at this moment.

Mr. Harrison went on to explain that any further outbursts from Rachel would result in her suspension. Amelia calmly thanked him for the phone call and hung up the receiver, letting out a deep sigh.

"Do you know how to add and subtract positive and negative integers?" Rachel asked Zac as he pulled his truck to a stop.

He had picked Rachel up after her detention and she hadn't said a word all the way home.

"Yes, as a matter of fact, I do," Zac answered. "I'm guessing that maybe you don't or you probably wouldn't be asking me. It doesn't seem like something you would be just waiting to brag about."

"Can you teach me?"

"Of course I can. Let's eat supper first and then we'll find our way through all the positive and negative stuff."

"Sir Isaac Newton, who invented calculus, had trouble with names to the point where he would sometimes forget his brothers' names," Amelia said as she sat down at the table across from Rachel and Zac, who were hard at work on Rachel's math homework. "I'm glad you asked Zac to help you and not me, Rachel. I'm still spinning just listening to all that positive, negative talk."

Rachel had driven by the ferry on her way to school every day but she hadn't been on it since Mrs. Thompson had brought her to Walton Lake in August. Now, sitting high in Zac's truck as they headed across to the mall to do some Christmas shopping, Rachel could see a row of bubbles all the way along as the ferry moved through the cold, grey water. Zac explained that the bubbles she could see were from an underwater system that kept the ferry track from freezing.

"I think I'll buy Amelia a pair of earrings," Rachel announced. "I want to find earrings with flowers on them, pansies maybe."

"That sounds like a good idea," Zac said. "I often have a hard time deciding what to get her. She always surprises me, even though I'm the one that does all the shopping. Last year she ordered carved knobs for my kitchen cupboards from the Lee Valley catalogue and she got Terry Fullerton to pick me up a pair of new chainsaw pants. I think I'll get her a new sweater. That old brown one she wears needs to go to the rag bag. She always thinks of other people, but never thinks about getting herself new stuff."

Rachel sat quietly, staring out the truck window as they got onto the highway. She thought about her reaction when she'd seen Amelia for the first time. The lumps on her face had scared her and she'd found them hard to look at. She remembered the first time she'd seen Amelia in her bathing suit and how she'd gagged at the sight of her bare back.

She broke the silence with the question that had been eating her up for months. "What's wrong with her face, Zac?"

"I wondered when you would ask about that," he said. "Some kids ask right away. Travis asked Amelia the minute he got out of the car. He asked her if whatever was wrong with her face was contagious."

"I never thought that, but I thought it was gross. At first I tried not to look at her face."

"She has the disease NF1, which stands for Neurofibro something. I don't even try to pronounce it. It causes tumours to form under her skin."

"Like cancer?" Rachel asked.

"Not exactly. They aren't cancerous, but they come in clusters and they never clear up completely. She gets them on her neck and back, too, but usually she covers those up with her clothes so no one can see them."

"I made up a name for her when I first saw her," Rachel admitted. "In my head I called her 'Warty.' The lumps on her face gave me something to hate her for, and when I called her that I could convince myself of how disgusting she was." She spoke slowly now, trying to keep the emotion from her words. "It was the same with the twins and Raymond. I wanted to hate them, so in my head I called the twins 'Tweedle Dee' and 'Tweedle Dum' and I called Raymond 'Balloon Boy.'"

Zac pulled into the mall parking lot and turned the truck off. A few seconds hung in the air before he spoke. "I was really mean to Amelia when I first came, too," he said, slowly and deliberately. "I hit her once and told her to get her filthy leper's face away from me."

Rachel couldn't imagine Zac ever hitting anybody. It was even harder to believe that he'd ever given Amelia a hard time. He was so respectful of her now and helped her in so many ways. *Maybe there's hope for me, too,* Rachel thought.

"I'm going to buy Raymond a guitar," Zac said. "He'll drive us all crazy with it, but he's really musical. I know a guy that will give him lessons. Do you want to go in on it with me?"

"Sure," Rachel said, relieved for the change in subject.

"I don't know what to buy for Chelsea and Crystal," Zac continued. "I don't know how to pick clothes out for little girls. Can you help me with that?"

"Definitely."

"Okay, then. Let's go get some serious shopping done. How about we start by buying you some winter boots? Those orange sneakers won't hold up very long in this snow!"

Rachel placed her shopping bags on the floor of her closet. She'd actually been able to find a pair of earrings with pansies on them for Amelia, and hadn't even minded paying almost half her chore money for them. She'd gone in on the guitar for Raymond with Zac, but he had refused to take much money, and she'd found a Barbie Cruise Ship for Chelsea and Crystal. But the thing she was happiest about was being able to buy Zac a hooded sweatshirt without him seeing her. The one he had now was just about worn out, and he was always saying how great a hood was to keep his neck dry when he drove the tractor under tree limbs heavy with snow.

Rachel hadn't received any mail since she'd arrived at Walton Lake—or in any of her other foster homes, for that matter—so when she got the mail from the mailbox two weeks before Christmas and found an envelope addressed to her she had no idea who it could be from. She held the envelope up, studying both sides. The postmark said Golden, BC. The Walton Lake address had been printed on the front of the envelope under Rachel's name, which was written in fancy cursive lettering. There was no return address in the left-hand corner, but a sticker sealing the flap on the back of the envelope read: "From the desk of Audrey Anderson." The name Audrey Anderson meant nothing to Rachel. She looked at the letter for a few more seconds and then headed into the house and upstairs to her room.

Rachel sat down on the edge of her bed, opened the envelope, and pulled out a piece of bright pink paper. As she unfolded it, the first lines of the letter jumped out at her:

Dear Rachel,
My name is Audrey Anderson and I am your grandmother.

Rachel hadn't even made the connection. She knew her father's name was Donald Anderson, but it had been so long since she had heard his name spoken it hadn't occurred to her that this letter might be from someone related to him. Her mom had mentioned her dad's name every once in a while, and she'd always said the same thing about him: He wasn't able to be a husband or dad and had left after Caleb was born so that he could get some help. She'd always hoped that maybe some day he would be well enough to be with them. Rachel had never understood what her mom had meant and had long given up hoping that her father would come back. She couldn't even remember what he looked like. They had always been just fine, the three of them. Even after the accident, Rachel had never believed for one minute that her father would ride back into her life and take care of her.

Rachel thought about going downstairs, throwing the letter in the woodstove, and pretending that it had never come. *What could a grandmother I've never met have to say to me?* she wondered. The grandmother she did know, her mom's mom, hadn't cared enough to keep in contact with her, let alone take care of her after the accident, so why would she expect anything more from this one?

Rachel refolded the paper, placed it back in the envelope, and tucked it between the mattress and box spring. Then she picked up her book bag and dug inside, looking for her science homework. She didn't have time to think about her father and grandmother right now. *Besides,* she thought, *it's not like my father and grandmother have spent much time thinking about me in the last thirteen years.*

Rachel picked up a wreath and straightened the bow. She was helping Amelia and the others decorate the house for Christmas. Raymond and Zac were stringing lights up in the second-storey windows and the twins and Amelia were sitting at the kitchen table making a garland of fir boughs to hang from the stairway banister. Rachel put her coat and boots on, grabbed the wreath, and stepped out onto the front veranda so she could hang it on the front door. As she lifted the wreath up over the small window in the door, it made her think of the front door of her old house on Regent Street. That door had a half-moon-shaped window, with four panes of pie-shaped glass. Her mom had always made a big production of stringing the outside lights on the porch and hanging the wreath on the door. The last Christmas they'd had together, her mom had held Caleb up so that he could be the one to place the wreath on the nail above the window.

Rachel threw the wreath across the veranda. She had been trying all day to pretend that all this Christmas stuff mattered. And she had been pretending to be part of this makeshift family. *But I already had a family,* she thought to herself. *And I messed that up. After what I did to them, I don't deserve another one.* That last thought hurt the most.

Rachel walked quickly to the end of the driveway. She figured that if she kept walking, she could get to the main road before dark. She could hitchhike from the end of Walton Lake Road to the Westfield ferry, and then walk to the highway and try to get a lift to Fredericton. She didn't know where she'd stay when she got there. She just wanted to be close enough to see the lights of her old house. She needed to see the lights through that moon-shaped window and for a few minutes pretend that she still lived there and that what had taken her real family had never happened.

Snow started to fall and Rachel's pace slowed. Deep down, she knew she wouldn't go, and besides that she knew that getting there would never fix anything. Whoever lived in that house now was not her family. She was a kid with no family and nothing would ever change that—not her old house, not Amelia, and certainly not Donald or Audrey Anderson.

Social Studies was the last class before noon. Mr. Williston was standing at the front of the classroom, droning on about an assignment they were going to work on this week. Rachel wasn't paying the least bit of attention. She was completely immersed in the novel she was reading, which was concealed inside the textbook propped open on her lap.

"Sorry to bother you, Miss Garnham," Mr. Williston said. "But I think you should be paying attention to the instructions for an assignment that is going to be worth 50% of your December mark. Maybe you could come up to the board and fill in some spaces to show us what I just explained to the class?"

Rachel looked up at the diagram that Mr. Williston had drawn on the board. The title was "Family Tree." Mr. Williston printed Rachel's name in the oval in the middle and then walked toward her, passing her the chalk.

What happened in the next few minutes was a blur to Rachel. She was now sitting in the principal's office while he talked to Amelia on the phone. He was using words like "meltdown," "rage," "unacceptable behaviour," and "suspension."

Once he finished his phone call, Mr. Harrison told Rachel that she was suspended until after the holidays. She would have to meet with the guidance counsellor and someone from the district office before she would be allowed back in school. He made it very clear that he would not have a student in his school who was a danger to others.

"Someone could have been seriously hurt when you threw your chair," he said. "I will not have that kind of violent behaviour in my school!"

Rachel hadn't really thrown her chair. She had sat, not moving, while Mr. Williston had kept telling her to get up and fill in the spaces on the board. As she'd sat there, not responding, Mr. Williston had become more and more angry, yelling at her and asking her what made her think she didn't have to do the assignment. Then he'd grabbed the back of her chair and rocked it, trying to force Rachel to get up. When she'd stood up, the chair had gone flying. Rachel had run out of the classroom and was almost out the front door of the school when the principal had stopped her.

"Miss Walton is sending her neighbour to come and get you," the principal told Rachel. "You should be more considerate of her. You know she can't come pick you up. Besides, she has her hands full with the others. You are old enough now to know how to behave." Rachel just stared at him as he continued his rant. "I warned you the last time that your outbursts would not be tolerated. The kind of temper you just showed has no place in this school. And so close to Christmas."

Rachel stared straight ahead, not saying a word, but her mind was just about exploding with what she wished she could say.

"So close to Christmas," he'd said. *If only he knew what Christmas means to me!* Rachel thought angrily. She had held her breath to get through every Christmas for the last five years. Christmas in all those other homes just made remembering Christmas with Caleb and her mom harder to bear. This year at least she knew there would be no one getting so drunk that she would have to barricade her door to keep him out.

This year she had helped cut the tree and she and Raymond had dragged it into the front room last night. They had all helped trim it and Amelia had placed presents under it before they went to bed. She had seen presents there for her. She had a stocking with her name on it, too. Amelia had knit it and Rachel hadn't even seen her working on it.

"You should be more considerate of Miss Walton," Rachel repeated in her head angrily. *"She can't come get a foster child."* *He has no idea what Amelia can and can't do!* she thought to

herself. *"Old enough to behave."* *Old enough to know that I had nothing to put in a family tree diagram! No father, a dead mother, a dead brother, one grandmother who didn't want me, and another who lives on the other side of the country. No family equals no branches for a stupid tree.*

Rachel could feel tears starting to well up in her eyes, but there was no way that she was going to cry in front of Mr. Harrison. She sat just there silently, staring straight ahead, fighting back the tears, until Zac knocked on the door. The vice-principal walked her to her locker to get her stuff while the principal talked to Zac, probably warning him about the *dangerous offender* he was picking up.

They were almost home before Rachel said a word to Zac. He hadn't asked her anything since he'd picked her up—he'd just sung along to the radio as he drove. But when Rachel began to speak he reached over and turned the music off. "It wasn't my fault!" she cried. "Mr. Williston just kept going on about a stupid family tree, and I didn't know what to do." She continued on, her words coming out in a jumble between sobs. "I wasn't going to stand up and tell everyone I don't have a family, that I had nothing to put in my tree. It's nobody's business."

When they arrived in Amelia's driveway, Zac reached over and touched Rachel's arm. "I know," was all he said.

Amelia was sitting at the kitchen table when they entered. She stood up and took Rachel's backpack from her. "Take these lazy dogs down to the lake, would you?" she said. "You need some time by yourself. We're having your favourite Hawaiian Chicken for supper and I'll get you to help me make an apple crisp later on. We'll talk when you come back up."

The dogs followed Rachel out the door. There had been a light powder of snow the previous night, and the sun was glittering off the hill like a million tiny diamonds. The ice was solid now across the expanse of water and the boughs on the trees along the banks were covered with blankets of snow. It was very quiet; all Rachel could hear was the breathing of the dogs.

Rachel looked back up toward the house, thinking about what the principal had said about Amelia. He had been right about one thing: she should be more considerate towards her. Rachel vowed to herself that she would help Amelia as much as she could in the next few days so that having her out of school would not be a problem. For now, she would try to forget about having to go back in January, which would probably mean apologizing and admitting to being wrong. The unfairness of that didn't bother Rachel too much, because she was quite sure that when she talked to Amelia later, she would somehow understand. For the first time since she had lost her mother, she had someone who seemed to care about her, someone she could talk to. Two people, actually. She had Amelia and Zac, and that was more than she'd had since the day her mom and Caleb had left and never come home again.

When Rachel walked into the kitchen after her time at the lake, there was a sandwich and a glass of chocolate milk sitting on the table. She hung up her coat and sat down.

"You didn't have lunch, did you?" Amelia asked. "Your tuna sandwich was a bit smushed in your book bag so I made you another one. The snow looks beautiful, doesn't it? The snow banks were getting pretty dingy looking, but that dusting last night gave everything a nice new covering."

Amelia poured a cup of tea in her pansy cup and sat down

across from Rachel. "Tell me what happened."

"I wasn't paying attention," Rachel started. "If I had been, I would have just copied the diagram off the board and none of this would have happened. I'm sorry I caused you all this trouble, Amelia. I didn't know what to do. Mr. Williston was so mad and all I could do was sit there while he got angrier. How could I go up to the board and in front of everyone admit that I didn't have a family? That my mom and brother are dead? That I don't have a father? I know his name and I could have put it down, but I don't even remember him. I know his mother's name is Audrey, but I don't know his father's name or if he even has brothers and sisters. I tried to wait it out and just sit there, hoping Mr. Williston would give up, but he just got madder and madder. There was no way I was going to cry in front of everyone and all I could think to do was get out of there."

"He should have known better than to put you on the spot like that," Amelia said, putting her hand on Rachel's shoulder. "You did nothing wrong. Although I suppose like you said if you hadn't been reading you wouldn't have been caught off-guard. But I'm sure that whatever you were reading was probably a whole lot more interesting than Mr. Williston's class is at the best of times."

"I didn't know what to do. I'll go back after Christmas and apologize. Maybe I could do the project about your family or maybe he could give me something else to do instead."

"You will apologize for not paying attention. That is all you have to apologize for. I expect an apology from Mr. Williston as well. He has a responsibility to know about his students and to be sensitive to their circumstances. When you came in September all the teachers were told about your background so that something like this wouldn't happen. I know your past is your business, but some things are necessary to share in confidence. This could have been prevented if just a bit of sensitivity and respect had been shown to you. I'll call Mr. Harrison tomorrow morning and discuss this with him. We will accept the suspension and you can enjoy a longer holiday. You can help me get all the Christmas cooking done and do the rest of my wrapping for me. You can help Zac get the Christmas groceries and stocking stuffers, except your own, of course. I'll just have to trust Zac to do that. Don't be surprised if you get several boxes of peanut brittle. That is Zac's favourite so he always buys an abundance of peanut brittle. Now finish up your sandwich and go to the root cellar for some apples. And put a stick or two in the furnace while you are down there, please."

When Rachel got into bed later that night, she took the pink writing paper from the envelope that she had put under her mattress and read her grandmother's entire letter.

Dear Rachel,

My name is Audrey Anderson and I am your grandmother. Your father Donald is my son. I never met your mom. I have only one picture of you and your brother that your mom sent me when you were three and Caleb was one. I only found out about a year ago that your mom and brother had passed away. I am very sorry for your loss.

Your father has had a very hard time of it for a lot of years. I don't know what your mother told you about him but one thing I can tell you is that he loved your mother and you and your brother very much. He was very upset when he heard about the accident. He heard about it from a man that he worked with in Fredericton. He took a really bad turn after that.

I know it must be a surprise to hear from me. I am sorry that I did not try to contact you sooner. For a long time I have wanted to talk to you and tell you that I think of you all the time. I always told myself that you had your other grandmother and that you didn't need me. When Donald's friend told him he thought that you were in foster care, I started trying to get in touch with you.

I would love it if you would write back to me. Maybe you could send me a picture of yourself.

Love,
Your Grandmother

Rachel tucked the letter back in the envelope, slipped it under the mattress, got into bed, and pulled up the covers, thinking about her grandmother's words. *Maybe there are some branches on my family tree, after all,* Rachel thought before falling asleep.

Chapter 5

Long Johns and Goose Feathers

Rachel and Amelia worked side by side all week, and the Christmas cookies, cakes, pies, and treats they had already produced seemed like enough for a small bakery. They had also trimmed every room in the house, made up Christmas baskets for several neighbours, and strung lights on the large spruce tree in the front yard.

Rachel could hardly contain her excitement about Christmas. After wrapping all the presents she had for everyone she had found a book of Christmas facts in the book room and read the whole thing trying to distract herself. The way she felt seemed too good to be true and a part of her worried that something would happen to ruin things or take away this feeling. She didn't care how many gifts were under the tree. Just the fact that presents with her name on the tags were mixed up with everyone else's under that beautiful bushy tree, and people who cared about her had put them there, was amazing to her. Zac had made her promise she wouldn't shake one of the boxes he had stuck in behind the others last night. He didn't want her to guess what it was. She thought of her Christmas last year, when some church group had dropped off a box of junk people had donated. Margaret had just pulled things out of the box, wrapped them in cheap ugly paper, and stuck their names on them. The first present Rachel had opened Christmas morning was a Toronto Maple Leaf travel mug without the top. Whatever the presents under the tree were this year, she was pretty sure she wouldn't be receiving somebody's cast-off "Life Begins at Fifty" T-shirt like she had last year.

Jodie was coming the day before Christmas Eve to stay for a week. Zac was coming for Christmas Eve supper and Amelia was going to make his favourite lobster chowder. He was going to come for breakfast and stockings and the opening of the presents on Christmas morning, too, and Roger and his girlfriend Leslie were coming for Christmas dinner.

When Jodie arrived, the twins carried her suitcase and a huge box of gifts into the house. Raymond and Rachel emptied the box and placed the packages under the tree.

"There's about ten presents for each of us," Raymond exclaimed as he came back into the kitchen and sat down at the table. Amelia and Jodie were already seated there, decorating gingerbread cookies.

"If you received all of the gifts sung about in the song Twelve Days of Christmas you would receive 364 gifts," Rachel said as she joined them.

"Oh no!" Jodie shuddered jokingly. "You've caught the trivia bug from Amelia!"

"That would be a lot of gifts, Rachel," said Amelia. "I don't think we would have room under the tree for that many gifts for each of us, not to mention the mess calling birds and

French hens might make. Speaking of hens, Raymond, can you please go out to the chicken shed and collect the eggs before they all freeze on us? I'll need quite a few eggs for the rest of the baking we still have to do."

The wind was cold as Jodie and Rachel walked down the hill toward the lake. Zac and Raymond had cleared a spot with the tractor for a skating rink and there was just a skim of light snow over the ice. For her hour, Rachel was going to clean off the rink and she was happy to have Jodie along to help her.

"Isn't it amazing how the lake seems different in some way every time you see it?" Jodie asked. "I used to try to come down at the same time every day for a few days in a row and take notice of how the lake was different each time. It might be the direction of the wind, the slant of the shadows, or the sounds I heard. I used to pretend that the lake changed each day just for me. I still find myself waking up some days and feeling a powerful urge to stand on this shore."

"I know," Rachel said as she slid the flat shovel along the edge of the plowed space. "In November I watched it start to freeze over and felt so sad about not having the water to watch, but every time I come down I see something new about the ice. We had a fire on the shore last Saturday night and, sitting around it, watching the sparks shoot into the air, I swear I could hear the water below. I pretended it was telling me it was waiting for me."

"We are pretty sappy about this lake aren't we?" Jodie laughed. "I think Amelia was brilliant to know that what we needed was time alone and a place to love. I think she also knows that this lake is the kind of place that is pretty hard not to fall in love with."

"Why did you have to come here?" Rachel asked. As soon as she'd said it, she quickly added, "You don't have to tell me. It is none of my business." She couldn't believe she was talking so freely with Jodie.

"That's all right," Jodie replied with a smile. "You can ask me anything you want to."

"Are your parents alive?"

"My dad is. My mom died a few years ago. For the longest time I wouldn't even call them my mom and dad because mothers and fathers are supposed to look after their kids. That was something my parents did not know how to do. God knows they knew what to do to have kids and had eight of them. My mom was pregnant with the last one when Social Services finally took us away. They took the baby as soon as she had him so he didn't have to live with—or should I say without?—what the rest of us did. He was adopted right away and he lives on Prince Edward Island with his family."

"What about the other kids?"

"The rest of us got put in foster homes all over the province. I'm not even sure where they are now. You'd think that having parents like we had would have made us closer, but it did just the opposite. We were like a litter of wild kittens, each one desperate to get what we needed to survive. I have not seen any of my brothers or sisters since the day Social Services took us."

"Was this your first foster home?"

"No, I had to mess up really badly to get sent here. Amelia gets the kids nobody else wants. Sorry, I guess I probably shouldn't say that to you."

"That's OK," Rachel said thoughtfully. "I know it's true. Nobody has wanted me all along, but I got worse with each home I went to. My social worker made it perfectly clear this was the last resort she had for me."

"Well, I'm really glad that you are here," Jodie said. "This is a good place for you and you are doing fine. Amelia told me about that thing at school and that was not your fault. Believe me, I could tell you some horror stories of some of the stuff I did at school when I first got here."

Rachel started shoveling a path to reach the dock, which she could barely see beneath the snow. A few minutes later she looked up and saw Zac and Raymond heading toward the lake, carrying their skates.

"I'll run up and get our skates," Jodie said.

Rachel went back to work, scooping up shovelfuls of snow, waiting for Jodie to get back.

Rachel pulled up a chair beside the woodstove and propped her nearly frozen feet on the oven door. She stirred the marshmallows into her hot chocolate and sipped the steaming liquid. Jodie stood beside her, flipping grilled cheese sandwiches in the cast iron frying pan.

"Do you guys want to come to my house tonight and help me trim my tree?" Zac asked as he dipped his grilled cheese in a dollop of ketchup on his plate. "I wasn't going to bother but there was a perfect little tree on the edge of the back field and I thought I may as well cut it and put it up. I even bought a few ornaments at the drug store yesterday."

"I have some ornaments that we didn't use," said Amelia. "You can have them. And I have extra lights, too. I'm glad you decided to put up your own tree. There is nothing like the smell of a tree in the house for the Christmas season. I can't imagine not having a real Christmas tree in the house. Did you know that Germany made the first artificial trees out of goose feathers that were painted green?"

Rachel added one more ladle of lobster chowder to each of the last two bowls and carried them into the dining room. Snow was lightly falling outside and it was a perfect Christmas Eve. The twins had set the table with a Christmas tablecloth and napkins, and Jodie had lit some candles and turned off the overhead lights.

"In Mexico wearing red underwear on New Year's Eve is said to bring new love in the upcoming year," Amelia said as Rachel set the steaming bowls of chowder in front of Zac and Jodie.

"Well, I've got red long johns," Zac replied. "Now I just have to wear them on New Year's Eve and wait for love to find me. I hope whoever she is she can make lobster chowder as delicious as you do, Amelia."

Rachel looked at the faces around the table in the glow of the candlelight. She thought back to a point earlier in the day, when she had started crying for no reason. Raymond come around the corner of the chicken shed and ambushed Zac with snowballs. His laughter as Zac ran after him had sounded like Caleb's and she'd found herself standing there, watching them with tears streaming down her cheeks.

She and Caleb had built a snow fort in the backyard of their house on Regent Street. The next day Caleb had hid in it, waited until Rachel came out of the house, and surprised her with a volley of snowballs. He had laughed so hard and run toward the house, trying to get his snow pants off quickly so he didn't pee his pants. Their mom had met them at the door, holding the angel that they always put on the top of their tree. Rachel remembered her mom hollering at Caleb as he ran by her with his snow pants down around his knees, his snowy boots dripping puddles down the hall as he stomped toward the bathroom. It had been Christmas Eve, their last Christmas Eve, and the last Christmas Eve that she'd had a family. *Until now,* she thought.

Rachel's favourite gift had been the snowshoes. Now, as she trudged through the snow, lifting each snowshoed foot carefully as she tried to keep up with Zac and Jodie, she thought back to three mornings ago when she had opened her presents. It had been a chaotic morning, with wrapping paper strewn everywhere and the twins and Raymond announcing everything they got with excitement as they'd opened their presents. Amelia had passed out the presents, trying to keep it so that everyone always had something to open. She hardly opened any of hers until everyone else was finished. When she had opened her gift from Rachel, Amelia had gone right to the bathroom mirror and put the pansy earrings on, saying how beautiful they were.

Rachel had opened her gifts quietly, enjoying the anticipation as she slowly pulled the wrapping off of each one. She was completely awed by the pile of things in front of her when she was done. When she'd opened the gift from Zac, the box was empty. She was confused, especially since he had made such a big deal about hiding it so she wouldn't shake it. She found a note taped on the inside of the box that said her real gift was in the barn behind a bale of hay. Everyone had put their coats and boots on to follow her to the hay loft to find her present. The snowshoes had been wrapped in bright snowman paper with a big red bow, and Zac had taken the time to draw snowshoes on the bottom of each of the snowmen.

Rachel had been embarrassed that she didn't have a clue how to put the snowshoes on. At first she'd been really self-conscious of the clumsy way she'd walked with them once she got them strapped to her boots. But she was finally getting the hang of it now and she hadn't fallen over for at least ten minutes. She came into a clearing, where she could see Zac and Jodie sitting on a pile of logs. Jodie was unpacking the lunch Amelia had made for them and Rachel could only imagine what delicious stuff she had crammed into the backpack. She sat down on the log pile and Jodie passed her a turkey sandwich.

"I hope we weren't going too fast for you," Jodie said as Zac passed Rachel a mug of hot chocolate.

"No, I'm okay," Rachel answered between bites of her sandwich.

"If we keep taking this road we'll come out behind the lake," Zac said, pointing to a clearing through the thick stand of trees. "I haven't had the tractor down there since our last big snowfall, so it should be good snowshoeing. It is quite a ways, but we could come out and end up at Amelia's instead of backtracking and finishing up at my house."

Jodie passed out cinnamon-sugared donuts. "I think I'll head back to your place to get my car. I told the twins that I would take them for pizza and bowling tonight. My vacation is going so fast and I want to get everything I planned done. Rachel and I are going for a spa day tomorrow, aren't we?"

"Yup," Rachel said with a smile.

Zac finished his donut and bent down to put his snowshoes back on. "Ah, a spa day. I'm taking Raymond to his first guitar lesson tomorrow, or I might ask to come with you. I could sure use a pedicure," he laughed. "Too bad we couldn't get Amelia to go. Wouldn't it be nice to see her pampered after all the work she did getting ready for Christmas?"

"I know," Jodie replied. "I would ask her but I know she wouldn't come. I'll bring her back that shampoo she really likes. It amazes me how she can keep so content when she never leaves home. She's harder on herself than anyone else would ever be."

Rachel drank the last bit of hot chocolate from her cup and set it in Jodie's backpack. As she strapped on her snowshoes she thought about Jodie's words: *She's harder on herself than anyone else would ever be.*

"The thing about my Macaroni Delight is that it's never exactly the same two times in a row. I throw whatever I can find in it," Zac explained as he shook a spice bottle over the ground beef he was cooking. Zac had met the kids at the bus and brought them to his house for supper because Amelia wasn't feeling well.

Rachel was chopping red and green peppers and onions. Raymond and the twins had gone out to the sheep pen hoping to find a ewe giving birth, even though Zac had told them it would be a month or so before the ewes began lambing.

"What if Amelia has to go to the doctor?" Rachel asked. She had noticed Amelia's cold getting worse and had heard her coughing a lot last night.

"Doctor Hollway will come to the house if we need him to," Zac answered. "A couple of years ago she had pneumonia and he came and wrote her a prescription. She doesn't get sick very often but I told her today that if she wasn't better by tomorrow I would call him to come again. She wasn't too keen on that."

"Amelia doesn't like anyone making a fuss over her, does she? But she's always thinking of other people. When Mrs. Fullerton was sick last week, Amelia sent her meals for four days. She is probably the most unselfish person I have ever met."

"I certainly agree with that. I had to force her to stop what she was doing this afternoon and go to bed. It made me think of the first few weeks after I came to live with her. She had to change the dressings on my burns and I would scream and fight her."

"Your burns?" Rachel asked as she put the paring knife down and turned toward where Zac was standing. All Zac had ever told her about coming to Amelia's was that he was eleven when he came. She didn't know anything about why he was put in foster care.

Zac kept cooking. He didn't look at Rachel as he reached over for the pile of chopped peppers and onions and added them to the frying pan.

"I was burned on my back and left arm. I had been in the hospital for a few weeks and when I was to be released I had nowhere to go so they brought me to Amelia. There had just been my dad and me. Put that macaroni in the pot would you, please? My dad died in the fire."

Rachel didn't know what to say. She was well aware of the awkward silence that always hangs in the air after you tell someone your parent is dead. She just stood there, silently waiting for Zac to continue or change the subject.

After a minute or so of silence, Zac spoke again. "It took me too long to jump. I was afraid and I stood there crying. Dad kept telling me I could do it and he forced me through the window. The roof collapsed just as I jumped from the windowsill and I got burned on my back and shoulder. My dad was knocked down and didn't make it. Amelia got me through those first few weeks and months."

Rachel stood stirring the macaroni, knowing there was nothing she could say to Zac that would take away his pain.

Two days later Rachel set Amelia's supper tray down and sat on the chair beside her bed. "Finally I'm getting some real food," Amelia laughed, stabbing a piece of chicken with her fork. "I hope I don't see tomato soup again for a good long time. And that disgusting medicine Dr. Hollway gave me, I'll be glad when I've taken the last of that. You kids have been great, though. The way you've been taking care of me, you'd think I was royalty."

"You would've done the same for any one of us," Rachel said. "Zac did most of the work."

"Zac's been amazing. He has waited on me hand and foot during the day. He brought me tea this afternoon, and he decorated the tray like he was serving tea at the Empress Hotel. I could almost picture myself sitting in the dining room of the Empress, having tea and scones."

"Where is the Empress Hotel?" Rachel asked.

"It's in Victoria, BC. It was built in 1908 and at the time it was the grandest of all the hotels. For many years it didn't even have a sign above the front entrance and, as a worker erected a sign years later, he was quoted as saying, *'Anyone who doesn't know this is the Empress shouldn't be staying here.'* In 1965 there was a debate about tearing it down but in 1966 they did a $4 million renovation that they dubbed 'Operation Teacup' and in 1989 they did an additional $45 million restoration."

"It sounds amazing," Rachel said. "I'd love to see it someday. But in the meantime, why don't I go perform my own Operation Teacup? The twins made your tea. I'll go get it and bring it up to you."

"Thanks," said Amelia, "but I think I'll get my lazy self out of bed and come downstairs to have my tea. This old house might not be as elegant as the Empress Hotel, but I'll be happy to see the rest of it. I've had enough of these four walls in the last few days."

The second letter came in mid-January. As soon as Rachel saw it in the mailbox she knew it was from Audrey Anderson. The beginning of it read like a tourist brochure for the town of Golden. Obviously Audrey Anderson had needed to really stretch to think of anything to write to a granddaughter she didn't even know. Apparently Golden had a population of 4,100. One of those 4,100 was Rachel's father. The town was 262 kilometres west of Calgary. *So what!* Rachel thought to herself. *Walton Lake road is about a million kilometres east of Calgary. Who cares?*

The letter went on to tell Rachel about all the exciting things there were to do in Golden: white water rafting, Heli skiing, snowmobiling, and hiking. Golden was nestled between two mountain ranges, the Purcell Mountains and the Rocky Mountains, in a place called Kicking Horse Country. *What is she, a travel agent or something?* Rachel wondered. *Is she trying to sell me a trip to Golden?* She read on to learn that Audrey Anderson lived next door to a place called "A Quiet Corner Bed and Breakfast" which was run by her friends Owen and Winnie Johnston. She sometimes made cinnamon buns for them. The whole first page of the letter was trivial information like this.

The second page was mostly about her father. Apparently he lived in a facility called "Top of the World Ranch Treatment Centre." He was a drug addict and was trying to deal with his addiction. Audrey said that he was holding on to the dream of someday seeing his daughter and being someone she could be proud of.

Rachel read that line several times. As far as she was concerned, there was nothing about Donald Anderson that she was proud of and for sure she was nothing for him to be proud of either.

In the last paragraph Audrey Anderson asked again if

Rachel would please write back to her and send her a picture. She also said that more than anything she prayed every day that she would get to meet Rachel. She hoped that someday Rachel could come to Golden and see her father and meet the rest of her family.

Rachel balled up the pages of the letter in her fist. *How does Audrey Anderson think I'm going to get all the way to British Columbia?* she wondered. *And what good is having a family all the way across the country? What good is having a family anyway when one wrong choice can take them away from you forever?*

It was Saturday morning, and Rachel and Jodie were heading to the city to do some shopping. Rachel had finally admitted that she needed to buy some new clothes. Even her orange sneakers were too small to wear. Before leaving, Rachel had put one of her school pictures in an envelope, wrote Audrey Anderson's name and address on the front, and licked the flap shut.

"Can we stop and get a stamp so that I can mail a picture to my grandmother?" Rachel asked.

She had told Jodie over Christmas that she had gotten a letter from her father's mother and told her about the second letter when it came. She hadn't told her much about what the letters had said except where they lived and what their names were. She definitely hadn't mentioned that her father was a drug addict or that her grandmother had invited her to come to Golden.

"Of course," Jodie said. Rachel had expected Jodie to start asking all kinds of questions about her grandmother, but she didn't. Rachel was relieved for the silence, and sat staring out the car window as they drove on.

"Do you remember Amelia ever leaving home?" Rachel broke

the silence while she and Jodie were waiting in line for the ferry. "Have you ever asked her to go anywhere?"

"Nope," Jodie said. "I really wanted her to go to my graduation when I graduated from Business College, but I knew she wouldn't go, so I didn't even ask her."

"Was she born with those tumours on her face?"

"No, they started coming out when she was in her early twenties. She was actually quite beautiful when she was young. Did you know that she was Miss Saint John in 1975? I found her sash one time when I was getting something from her room, and when I asked her about it she showed me a newspaper clipping."

"I hardly even notice her face anymore. I don't understand why she's so hard on herself. Why do you think she cares so much what other people think?"

"That's a good question. She has helped so many kids find their confidence and make the best out of the crappy situations they found themselves in. She certainly helped me to reshape the image I had of myself. I don't know why she hasn't been able to do that herself."

"Maybe she's been so busy worrying about everyone else's problems that she hasn't had a chance to think about her own," Rachel said thoughtfully. "Or maybe she's afraid to, and no one has tried to help her the way that she's helped us."

The third letter arrived on Groundhog Day. Rachel carried it straight from the mailbox to her room, and sat on her bed to read it.

Dear Rachel,

Your picture is beautiful. Thank you very much for sending it. You look a lot like your Aunt Victoria, your father's youngest sister. You have another aunt named Patricia. We would all love to meet you. I gave a copy of the picture to your father and he was thrilled to get it. He has it framed in his room. He is doing quite well in recovery and we are very hopeful that he'll continue making progress. He would like to write a letter to you but he wanted me to ask you first if it was all right. You can let me know if you would like to hear from him. I know it is very difficult after all these years. I hope you are doing well in your foster home. I would love to know more about your foster family, your school, and friends.

The letter had three more paragraphs. Rachel finished it, and then reread the first paragraph over and over. She looked like someone. People had always said how much Caleb looked like their mom, but no one had ever compared Rachel to her mom or Caleb. Her colouring and facial features were very different. She looked like her Aunt Victoria. She didn't even know until now that she had an Aunt Victoria.

After spending a long time poring over the letter, Rachel went to the bathroom and closed the door. She stood in front of the rectangular mirror and brushed the long brown hair away from her brownish-green eyes. The picture ID card that her first social worker had made for her said her eyes were hazel. She remembered holding that card, wondering why she needed something saying who she was when there was no one in the world who cared, no one that she belonged to. Hazel eyes. Aunt Victoria's eyes, maybe. And maybe Aunt Victoria had the same thin top lip, too.

Audrey, Donald, Victoria, Patricia. A family she was part of. Golden, BC. A place where she might belong.

Chapter 6
The Start of a Plan

March break was a wet, cold week, but Rachel was glad for the holiday. Jodie took two days off from work and came up to stay on Wednesday night.

"I got another letter from my grandmother," Rachel said as she and Jodie watered a line of seed pots on a table in the parlour.

"Did she get your picture?" Jodie asked.

"Yep," Rachel answered. "She wants me to go out to visit her this summer."

"Wow!" Jodie said, looking truly excited for Rachel. "Is she going to pay for you to fly there?"

"She probably would, but I'm not going to ask her," Rachel answered. "I'm going to ask Amelia to drive me to British Columbia."

"You're going to ask Amelia to *what?*" Jodie stopped watering and sat down on the sofa, waiting for Rachel to tell her more.

"You know how Amelia always talks about her dream to someday have tea at the Empress Hotel?" Rachel started.

"Well, I don't think I could get her to go all that way just for tea, but if I tell her I really need to go see my family, she might force herself to go. So I'm going to ask her to take me to BC to meet my grandmother and see my father this summer, and then afterwards, since we'll already be in the province, we can keep going all the way to Victoria to have tea at the Empress."

Jodie didn't say a word. She just sat on the couch processing what Rachel was telling her.

"I think I could put on a really convincing act that would make Amelia think I desperately need to connect with my grandmother and father," Rachel continued. "I thought maybe Zac could fix up a car for us to take. I know Amelia can't leave the other kids alone, but I thought you might be able to come and stay with them. And Zac is around to help, too. You get holidays don't you?"

"You've been giving this a lot of thought, haven't you?"

"I have," Rachel said. "Ever since I got the second letter from my grandmother, I've been wondering what she's like, and what my dad is like. I keep picturing Golden and thinking of it as a place that I have always needed to go, a place where I might belong. I can even picture my dad, though I have no idea what he really looks like. I see him sitting waiting for me on a bench beside a sign that says "Top of the World Ranch." I know this is crazy and Amelia will never go for it, but I can't get it out of my head."

"Well it's definitely crazy," Jodie said. "But I'll do my best to help you. We'll have to take this in baby steps, though. We'll have to work on convincing Amelia that she can leave Walton Lake first, and then work our way up to the BC idea. None of us have ever tried to get Amelia to leave, and the more I think of it the more I think we have just been selfish to let her get stuck here. I think maybe we all just wanted to make sure she would always be there when we needed her. That's crazy, when you think of it."

Zac was finishing off his second plate of baked beans and ham. Crystal and Chelsea had already cleared the other dishes off the table and everyone was anxious for a game of dominoes.

"I'm going to take a run up to the house first and check on that old ewe," Zac said as he sopped up some bean juice with his bread. "I expect her to lamb anytime and she lost twins last year, so I've been keeping a close eye on her. I'll beat you all at a game when I get back."

"Rachel and I will come with you," Jodie said, giving Rachel a little wink. The girls had decided to tell Zac about their plan to see if he would help them execute it, and they'd been waiting for a chance to speak to him alone.

"It would cost about 200 bucks for a clutch and about 100 bucks for filters and new brake pads, and I need to do a bit of body work on it for it to pass inspection," Zac said.

After checking on the ewe, Jodie, Rachel, and Zac had gone to Zac's house for some hot chocolate. They were now sitting at the kitchen table discussing the possibility of Amelia driving to BC. Last year, Zac had purchased an old GMC Jimmy to fix up and sell, but it had been sitting untouched in his garage ever since. As soon as he'd heard Rachel's plan, he'd offered to fix it up so Amelia could use it for the trip.

"About 500 bucks should do it and then Amelia would have to register it and put insurance on it," Zac explained. "And she might have to take a test to renew her license since it has been so long since she's driven."

Rachel nodded, trying to hide her excitement.

"Getting a vehicle ready will be the easy part," Zac added. "Persuading Amelia that she can leave home, let alone go all the way across the country—that sounds next to impossible."

"We won't know unless we try, Zac," Rachel pleaded, more to convince herself than to sell Zac on the idea.

"Rachel's right," Jodie said. "By never questioning Amelia's refusal to leave the house, we've let her tell herself year after year that she's right to not let strangers see her. She needs to see that what strangers think is not important. She needs to know that the people who love her don't believe her world should be limited to Walton Lake. We are going to do it, I just know it. And you, Rachel, will be the kid that finally changes the story that Amelia has told herself for thirty years."

"I hope so," Rachel said, suddenly feeling the weight of what they were about to do.

It was almost April, and the snow was starting to melt. Rachel was busy cleaning the barn when she heard Jodie's car drive up. She was bursting to run up to her and bring the plan up right away. They were going to start phase one today. Jodie was going to start mentioning how nice it would be for Amelia to be able to visit Jason and Megan in Calgary this summer and see the new baby. It had been Jodie's brilliant idea to give Amelia this reason to drive across the country.

Jodie was just going to drop a few hints at first—not enough to make Amelia suspicious. It was going to be a slow process, not something they would spring on her all at once. They had to plant the seed of the idea first and let it grow, and slowly. She had been firmly rooted at Walton Lake for thirty years, and it was going to take a long time to for her to come around to the idea of leaving.

Zac and Jodie talked to Raymond, Chelsea, and Crystal

to enlist their help with the plan as well. Zac thought they would need some time to come to terms with the idea of Amelia leaving them for what would likely be almost an entire month. Raymond, Chelsea, and Crystal had seemed fine with the idea, though, and they'd all promised not to say anything to Amelia until the time was right.

During the next week, Rachel spent every spare minute at Zac's, watching him as he worked on the Jimmy. She had helped him spread the body fill on some of the rust spots and she'd taped newspaper on the windshield and windows so that Zac could spray the touchup paint. It certainly didn't look brand new, but it would be good enough to pass inspection and reliable enough to make such a long trip.

When she'd visited last week, Jodie had told Amelia she'd heard from Jason and he'd told her that Megan was doing well and they were looking forward to the new baby coming. Jodie had also told Amelia that Jason had said he wished Amelia could come there. This wasn't all completely a lie. Jodie had called Jason and told him the plan, and he had agreed that it would be wonderful if Amelia would come there to visit. He was well aware that she hadn't left home for thirty years and after Jodie talked to him about it, he was quite enthusiastic to help by working on Amelia in his own way.

On Tuesday morning Raymond asked Amelia if she would come to his classroom on April 12 for his book project presentation. For a moment Rachel had panicked, thinking if Amelia said no, Raymond might blow the plan by blurting out that Rachel planned on asking her to go all the way across the country. But he hadn't said anything like that. He'd just asked her to come as if she had attended every other thing that had ever gone on at the school.

Amelia's reaction had surprised them all. She hadn't seemed shocked or taken aback, and she hadn't said anything about never leaving home. Instead she'd just answered that she would think about it. They'd all just finished breakfast quietly.

"Dolphins don't automatically breathe; they have to tell themselves to do it," Amelia broke in as she began clearing off the table. "You guys hurry up now and get yourselves down to the bus stop."

Amelia stood in front of the small rectangular mirror hanging over the bathroom sink. She rarely looked in that mirror other than to quickly brush her hair or to check to see if something was caught in her teeth. Occasionally she would see the bumps on her face after days of forgetting they were even there. She stood today studying her face and neck. She was getting old. Her face was wrinkled and her colouring was mottled. She could see a strong resemblance to her grandmother. She wished she could talk to her grandmother right now.

Part of her knew that if her grandmother had lived longer she never would have accepted her decision to exile herself the way she had. She remembered that even in her grandmother's last days, when her strength was all but depleted, she would scold Amelia for being so critical of herself. *How has so much time gone by since then?* she wondered. *And how has it gotten so easy to just stay in my small world and let other people come to me?*

Raymond asked her to go to his classroom, a classroom that he finally wanted to be in. It would be wonderful to go and watch him present his project with the other kids. How could she refuse him? And Jodie had told her that Jason wanted her to go out to visit him. Wouldn't it be wonderful to see Jason, Megan, little Logan, and the new baby?

Amelia stared at the contours of her face. No beauty there now, just an aging woman with bumps on her face. Harmless bumps that she had made into mountains with her own vanity. Mountains out of molehills, her grandmother had always said.

"Did you know that in Bellingham, Washington, it's illegal for a woman to take more than three steps backwards while dancing?" Amelia asked as she swept beside the wood box.

Zac grabbed Jodie and pretended to dance her across the kitchen floor. The twins giggled as he attempted a dramatic dip. Zac and Jodie's eyes met for a second, and they both blushed. Zac quickly straightened Jodie back up and bowed toward Chelsea. "May I have this dance, young lady?" he asked her.

Rachel stood at the kitchen sink, straining the pail of milk Raymond had just brought in. Milking the cow was something she had so far avoided doing. She had watched while Amelia did it and there was no way she was touching that part of a cow. Even just the thought of drinking the watery-looking milk she was straining was disgusting to her. She only drank real milk, the milk that came in a carton.

"Can you drive me to the school tomorrow?" Amelia asked Zac as he whirled Chelsea around the room.

Rachel almost knocked the funnel off the top of the glass bottle she was filling. Since the morning Raymond had asked Amelia to go to his presentation, nothing more had been said. Raymond had been working on his book report project for the last few days, and with Zac's help he had built an amazing model of a castle, but the whole time they'd been working Amelia hadn't said a word about going to the presentation.

"Sure," Zac answered calmly as he led his dance partner

back to her seat. "Do you want me to take your project in the truck, Buddy?" he asked Raymond. "It is pretty big to take on the bus."

"Sure," Raymond said. "That would be great!"

"Can you invite more than one person to the presentation?" Zac asked. "I would love to be there when the other kids see the drawbridge that really works."

The look on Raymond's face almost brought tears to Rachel's eyes. He looked like he would burst with pride and excitement. Jodie grabbed his arms and led him across the kitchen dance floor. As they danced, he laughed so hard tears streamed down his face. Then Zac pulled Crystal to her feet and with an exaggerated flourish swooped her toward the makeshift dance floor.

"Imagine the dancing you all could do if there was actually any music!" Amelia laughed. "And don't bother asking me, Casanova. I've got work to do. Sunday night's supper won't make itself," she said as she went in to the pantry.

Amelia listened to the coffee drip into the pot. She was sitting at the kitchen table, enjoying the quiet stillness of the room. It was such a change from just a few minutes before, when everything had been a whirlwind of activity as the kids got ready to leave for school. She had not slept much the night before. She had woken from her brief sleep with a headache and a heaviness she rarely felt. When she asked Zac if he could drive her to the school last night, she had actually believed that going was something she could easily do. Since the day Raymond had asked her to go, she had been battling with her thoughts. Over and over she'd told herself it was time she let her fears go. She knew she had to make herself go out into the world. It seemed so ridiculous when she thought about it. She had hidden herself away for over thirty years. It had been a selfish and foolish way to handle her condition. It was insane. But no one had stopped her. No one had ever even confronted her about it. Raymond's one simple request had begun a dialogue that nothing else had ever forced her to have.

It had taken a long internal battle, but she'd convinced herself she could do this. Then the insomnia of last night had come and all she'd been able to think about was that she could not take her hideous face out in public. She'd kept telling herself she was perfectly fine right here. That she had done good work with the kids over the years. That she wasn't hurting anyone by staying here. She knew, of course, that the stone she felt in the pit of her stomach was the weight of all the years she had anchored herself here by believing those thoughts.

Amelia poured herself a cup of coffee and sat back down. She knew that the person she would hurt the most today if she stayed home would be Raymond. She knew deep down that she had to do this for him. She resolved that she would be ready when Zac came at 12:30. She would step out the door, get into Zac's truck, drive out Walton Lake Road with him to the school, and walk right into Raymond's classroom.

Rachel spent most of the first class after lunch in a nervous distraction. She sharpened her pencil about ten times, each time trying to linger long enough at the window to see if Zac's truck was in the parking lot. Somehow she had missed the couple of minutes it would have taken him to park it and walk across to the main door, so when she finally did see his truck she wasn't sure whether Amelia had come with him. All morning she'd had a feeling that Amelia would change her mind. She had seemed so quiet at breakfast time and her eyes had looked heavy and sad.

Rachel didn't think Raymond had noticed that in all his excitement this morning. All he'd talked about on the way down the driveway was Amelia coming to his presentation. Rachel had known all along how incredibly disappointed Raymond would be if Amelia didn't come today, but she hadn't realized until now how upset she would be, too. If Amelia could actually leave today, the chances of her being able to go out again would be good, and the idea of her taking a trip across the country would not be absolutely unthinkable.

"I'm making supper tonight," Rachel announced as she walked through the front door after school. She had known as soon as she saw Raymond get on the bus that Amelia had been there. Raymond had sat in the front seat right behind Roger and talked cheerfully almost all the way home. He had still been talking as they'd walked all the way up the driveway.

"What are you going to make? Amelia asked.

"That chicken casserole with Stove Top dressing," Rachel answered. "I'll use the leftover chicken from last night. I'll make an apple crisp, too. We should call Zac to come for supper. Did you just get home? You should go have a nap. I'll do everything for supper. Raymond, fill the wood box, would you?"

Rachel could hear herself talking a mile a minute. For the first time in at least thirty years, Amelia Walton had left her farm. She wanted to hug Amelia, to ask her how it felt, to blurt out all she had been planning and ask her right now about the drive across the country. She wanted to say what a special occasion this was. She wanted to take Amelia's hands and dance her around the kitchen. This was a major break-through and Rachel was overwhelmed with the thought of it.

"Astronauts are not allowed to eat beans before they go into space because passing wind in a space suit will damage it," Amelia said as she headed upstairs. "You wouldn't catch me getting in a spaceship, or even an airplane for that matter. This old lady passes wind with her feet firmly on the ground."

Amelia's random fact quickly brought Rachel back to the reality around her. Rachel laughed out loud and thought to herself that it was a good thing she was trying to convince Amelia to drive across the country, because by the sound of what she had just said, getting her to fly *would* be impossible.

Rachel looked down at the paper in front of her. She had been working on the letter to her grandmother for at least an hour. She kept writing things and crossing them out. She wanted to tell Audrey Anderson some things about herself but some of it sounded so stupid when she wrote it.

Dear ~~Mrs. Anderson~~ ~~Audrey~~ Grandmother,

My name is Rachel Joy Garnham. ~~Garnham was my mother's name.~~ ~~My mother and Donald were never married, but you must already know that.~~ My birthday is July 15th and I will be 14 this year. I am in Grade 8. I go to Macdonald Consolidated School. It is an old building. It says 1904 over the front door. I have several different teachers and my favourite one is Mrs. White, my math teacher. I ~~have a lot of trouble with Math but I am getting better.~~ I came to live at this foster home in August. Amelia Walton is the woman who looks after us. ~~When I first came here I called her Warty.~~ ~~That was not very nice of me but she has a really bumpy face and I was really angry when I got here.~~ She has a farm and we all have to help with the chores. We live beside a lake. ~~The lake is called Walton Lake after Amelia's family.~~ There are three other kids here, twins named Chelsea and Chrystal and a boy named Raymond. ~~It took me awhile to get used to them but now I~~

A man named Zac lives down the road and he helps us a lot on the farm. He gets the groceries and stuff like that. ~~Amelia has not left home for a long time~~ He used to live here when he was a kid. Jodie lived here too. Jodie is our friend. She visits us a lot.

I would like to meet you and my two aunts sometime. ~~I am glad Dad~~ I am glad ~~Donald liked my picture~~ you gave my picture to your son. He can write to me if he wants to.

Rachel took another sheet of paper from her binder and recopied the parts of the letter she wanted sent to her grandmother. She thought carefully about how she would sign it, and then finally decided on:

Yours Truly,
Rachel

The sun was very warm for the first day in May. Rachel had slipped off her socks and sneakers and was dangling her feet off the side of the dock. The water was cold, but after a few minutes her legs had gotten used to it. The lake was still and the mid-afternoon sun was glistening on its surface. Rachel had already been here longer than her hour, but supper was going to be later tonight because Amelia had gone to Sussex with Zac to buy seeds for the garden. Amelia had been several places since the day she left to go to Raymond's classroom. She had gone to get groceries with Zac twice and had even gone to the Chinese restaurant in Quispamsis for supper with Jodie last week.

Rachel had given Amelia another letter to mail for her today. She had started talking to Amelia about her grandmother, her father, and Golden, BC. Her plan was to wait until the next letter arrived from Audrey Anderson and then tell Amelia that her grandmother really wanted her to go out and see them. She would seem uninterested at first and then begin to talk more and more about her family wanting her to visit them. Once she'd let that information percolate with Amelia for a while, she'd start mentioning that she'd like to go see them, too.

Jason had called Amelia the other night and even though Rachel hadn't heard his side of the conversation, she could tell he'd told her that he and Megan wouldn't be able to come east this fall. He had just started a new job and the new baby was due to be born in a few days. Jason's little boy, Logan, had talked to Amelia for a couple of minutes. Afterwards Jodie had really laid it on thick about how wonderful it would be for Amelia to see Jason and his family. She'd mentioned several times how thrilled Jason would be if Amelia was ever able to come out to see him. She also added that a vacation would be a well-deserved break after all the years she had devoted to caring for kids and running the farm.

Amelia was exhausted. She had dozed off a bit on the drive home, but she'd woken as Zac pulled onto their road. Her head was aching and she could feel the tension in the back of her neck. The feed store had been very busy, and she'd felt very self-conscious today, for some reason more than she had the other times she'd been out. It was if she could feel every bump and lump magnified on her face. Each time a person had looked in her direction her body had tightened and she'd turned away. She had gotten so self-conscious that she'd ended up going back to the truck before they had chosen all of the seeds, leaving Zac to finish the shopping.

"You should try driving the truck, Amelia," Zac said now as he pulled over to the side of the road. "You still remember how to drive, don't you?"

Amelia looked over at Zac as he turned the truck off and removed his seatbelt and considered what he was asking of her. "I suppose I could give it a try," she finally said. "I still have a license, you know. I've kept it renewed all these years because Social Services felt it looked better on the records that I had a valid driver's license in case of an emergency. They always overlooked the fact that there was no vehicle on the premises for me to drive."

Amelia opened her door and stepped out. The fresh air felt good and she let herself relax a bit as she climbed up into the driver's seat. She had not driven since the last time she drove the old Oliver tractor, but hopefully it was something one didn't forget. She fastened her seatbelt, stepped down on the clutch, and started the engine. And then she drove home.

Rachel was just reaching the top of the path from the lake when she saw Zac's truck coming up the driveway. She did a double take when she saw that Amelia was driving. Rachel ran up to the truck as Amelia came to a stop and opened the driver's side door with a smile, clearly showing her excitement at seeing Amelia behind the wheel.

Neither Amelia's expression nor her demeanour showed any signs of excitement or acknowledgement of what Rachel felt was a huge breakthrough in her progress. In Rachel's mind, she could clearly imagine Amelia driving the Jimmy out Walton Lake Road and onto the network of highways that would get them to Golden, BC. And more and more she was letting herself get a picture of her father greeting her with a look on his face that could change everything she now believed about herself.

"The Sears Tower in Chicago contains enough steel to build 50,000 automobiles," Amelia called out as she leaned into the back seat of the cab to get out the bag of seeds.

It was two weeks later when Rachel received a letter from Donald Anderson. He had enclosed a picture of himself holding a newborn baby, and by the date on the back of the picture Rachel knew that the baby was her. She was tightly wrapped in a striped pink hospital blanket and a small pink hat sat slightly sideways on her head. Her father looked scared to death, as if was afraid he would drop the little bundle he was holding. He was wearing a Toronto Blue Jays cap, an Alpine beer T-shirt, and blue jeans. His face looked dirty with the stubble of a growing beard. She could see what she assumed were her mother's legs in a part of the hospital bed shown in the foreground of the shiny square picture. The photo itself looked wrinkled, as if it had been in a pocket or jammed into a wallet.

Rachel sat the picture down on her bed and started reading the letter. It was handwritten on a piece of looseleaf paper. Her father wrote about how beautiful her mother had been. He said he had been very happy when both she and Caleb were born. He had told her five times that he loved her. He had used the word "sorry" eight times and used the word "shitty" when he'd talked about what kind of a father he had been. The last line of the letter was underlined. It said:

I thank God every single day that you did not die in that accident.

It was not a long letter, but by the end of it she was crying. After reading it over five times, Rachel carefully folded it back up and placed it under her pillow. Then she picked up the photo of her and her father and propped it up on her night table.

All four kids and Amelia were down at the lake, but only Rachel was determined to take the plunge into the still-cold water. Last week she'd read a news story about a woman who had the tradition of taking her first swim on the May long weekend, and for the past few days she'd been telling herself that no matter what the weather was on Saturday, she was going to start that tradition for herself. She had announced it at breakfast today and the others had made a big celebration of it. Amelia had made a picnic lunch for them and they had spread everything out on the shore. Rachel had waded in up to her knees, and everyone was cheering her on. Sam had run past her after his stick and splashed her as he went by, but getting in the water was still proving harder than she had imagined it would be. After all, she had been looking forward to this day since her last swim in September. *Just get it over with*, she kept telling herself.

Before Rachel took another step deeper, Bud barked and took off up the path. She looked up to see that he was running toward Jodie and Zac, who were both wearing their bathing suits. Rachel called out that she would wait for them.

"Charles Zibbleman swam for 168 consecutive hours in a pool in Honolulu in 1942," Amelia piped in as Zac and Jodie got closer. "Three years earlier, he swam the Hudson River from Albany to New York, a distance of 147 miles. Charles Zibbleman had no legs."

"I feel like I have no legs!" laughed Zac as he rushed into

the water. "This water is freezing them numb. But if Rachel wants to start a tradition today, we aren't being left out. Last one under is a dirty rotten egg!" he said.

Rachel dropped the pea seeds into the shallow ditch Raymond was making with the end of the hoe. After the time at the lake, everyone had gone straight to work, and now the garden was about three-quarters planted. Chelsea was coming along behind Rachel covering the pea seeds. A few rows over Amelia and Crystal were planting corn. Jodie and Zac were sitting together on the veranda, cutting up seed potatoes. Every once in a while Rachel could hear their laughter.

Rachel could feel her wet hair sticking to the back of her neck. The swim had been fantastic. Once she had taken the plunge and got over the initial shock, the water had been beautiful. Zac had beaten her and Jodie in, but they were just seconds behind him. It had felt so good to have them swimming with her. And she had not forgotten how to swim. All winter she had worried a bit about that, thinking she might not remember how or that her fear of the water might return. But she had done just fine and had swum quite a ways out with Zac and Jodie at her side. The others had cheered as if she had accomplished a world record just like Charles Zibbleman.

Amelia dropped the last corn seed. She stood up and looked over at the others. *Another garden being planted,* she thought, *the beginning of another growing season.* She felt so content. She had everything she wanted right here. It had been a good life and she could feel a certain pride for having kept this farm running and taken care of all of those kids over the years. Sometimes she felt like the progress the twins had made was too good to be true. They were a lot more talkative and open now, and she could see them coming out of their shells a little more every day. Seeing the smile that constantly covered Raymond's face as he worked around outside always made her heart swell. Rachel was doing all right, too, she thought. There had been no more issues at school and even though Rachel remained quiet and guarded, she seemed settled and less anxious. And every day Amelia grew prouder of the adults Zac and Jodie had become. Jason, too. It had been wonderful to talk to him the other day when he'd called to tell them about the baby being born. He had been over the moon with excitement about his new daughter, proudly telling her that they had named her Amelia. He had come a long way from the traumatized teenager who had come to her ten years ago.

Over the last few days she had thought a lot about how she felt the last time she had gone out, about the fear and self-consciousness that had almost paralyzed her at the seed store. She had told herself a few times since then that she had been right to stay here all those years and not expose herself to the judging looks of others. But standing here today, it occurred to her that the joy and privilege of being here was not hinged on the exile she had imposed on herself. In fact, her love of her home had become even clearer to her when she had finally let herself leave. She knew now that she had the choice. She could come and go and this place and this feeling would still be here for her when she got home. And no matter how it might seem, she knew that the feeling had nothing to do with how other people saw her.

"My grandmother wants me to go visit her this summer,"

Rachel said as she cut carrot coins into a pot of boiling water. Amelia stood next to her, peeling the potatoes. Rachel had been waiting for days to find the right opportunity to make that statement, and now that she'd put it out there she was dying to hear Amelia's response.

"Do you want to go?" Amelia asked, not taking her eyes off the potato she was peeling.

"Well, she really wants me to," Rachel answered nervously. "But she lives in British Columbia. It is not like it's just down the road. She really wants to meet me. My two aunts want to meet me, too. And my father wants to meet me. Well, he has already met me, of course, but he doesn't really know me. He would like to get to know me. I have cousins, too. And my grandmother says they want to meet me. I don't have a grandfather. He died before I was born. He has a sister in Revelstoke, though, and she also wants to meet me."

"Wow, that is a lot of people that want to meet you," Amelia said. "Do you want to go?" she asked again.

Rachel started to cry. She certainly hadn't planned on that. She had just planned on indifferently dropping the fact that her grandmother and other family members really wanted her to go. She wasn't ready to give any indication that *she* actually wanted to go. She wasn't even positive that she did. But when Amelia asked her if she wanted to go, the emotion had flooded through her and completely caught her off-guard.

Amelia put the paring knife on the side of the sink and turned toward Rachel. For the first time since her arrival nine months ago, Rachel reached out to Amelia and allowed herself to seek comfort in the woman's arms.

Supper was over, the dishes were done, and the table was set up for a game of dominoes. Everyone had just sat down to start playing when Amelia made the announcement to the others.

"We need to come up with a plan to get Rachel to British Columbia this summer. I'm going to go with her, and I am going to Calgary to see Jason and Megan on the way. I won't fly, but taking a train or a bus might be a possibility. Or I suppose I could drive, if I had a car."

There was a moment of stunned silence as the others at the table processed what Amelia had just said.

"Zac has the Jimmy he bought from Brad Campbell ready for the road again," Raymond finally offered as he looked up from his dominoes. "Maybe you could drive that."

"And maybe Jodie could stay with us while you're gone," Chelsea piped in.

"You could go have tea at the Empress Hotel, Amelia!" Chrystal chimed.

"Wow, those are great ideas!" said Amelia. "And you guys came up with them so quickly—almost as if you'd been thinking about them already! It seems like maybe there has been a bit of a secret mission going on here. Do you know where the saying 'Mum's the word' comes from, you secret keepers? It comes from the sound you make when you speak with your mouth shut tight. Mmmm. If you want to keep a secret, mummmm is the word to say. Apparently mum's been the word around here for a while."

Chapter 7
Going Down the Road

The month of June was busy with the preparations and work that needed to be done to get ready for Amelia and Rachel's trip. It hadn't taken long after Amelia's May long weekend announcement to get the ball rolling. Zac had driven the Jimmy into the yard the next day and assured Amelia that it was in good working order. Jodie had bought her seat covers for the two front seats. For two weeks Amelia had practised using the four-speed shift by driving in and out the road and up and down Zac's steep driveway. Then she and Zac had gone to Hampton and registered the truck in her name. The next day she'd driven the kids to school and she'd been driving it every day since.

Amelia was keen about the trip and realized it wouldn't be a short one if they were to drive all the way across the country. It had been difficult to convince her that she could leave the kids and the farm for a whole month, even though everything was running smoothly on that front. The garden was all planted and everything was up and growing. The new meat king chickens and turkeys had been picked up and the cow had birthed her calf.

Raymond and the twins had repeatedly told Amelia that they would be fine if she went. Jodie had somehow managed to get the whole month of July off work and was planning to stay at the farm for the entire time. Zac had assured Amelia that he would keep everything under control and that she deserved a vacation.

Amelia had called Sarah Thompson and asked her if there was any problem with her taking Rachel out of the province. She told Amelia that all it required was written permission from her as Rachel's social worker. She also said that she would be able to give them the July support cheque in advance so that it could be used to help with the trip's expenses.

Rachel was a bit overwhelmed with the way things were coming together so quickly, and as the time to leave got closer she found herself wondering why she had ever thought going to meet her family was a good idea. Even as she listened to the others reassuring Amelia that going was a great idea, she came up with a ton of reasons why it was the stupidest idea she'd ever had. But she kept those thoughts to herself. It wasn't until the day before they were planning to leave that it caught up to her and she finally told Jodie what she was really feeling.

"I wish the letter had never come from my grandmother," Rachel said as she and Jodie sat together by the lake late one Saturday afternoon at the end of June.

"Why do you say that?" Jodie asked.

"If I had never gotten her letter I still wouldn't know any-thing about her or my father and I never would have thought of leaving here. How can I do my part if I'm driving across Canada? And what about my hour at the lake? And I'm going to miss a whole month of swimming. What about the haying? What about the cooking and other chores? How are you guys going to handle things without having Amelia here? What if one of the twins falls out of the hayloft and breaks her arm? And what if I end up wanting to stay in BC.? What if I want to stay and nobody there wants me to?"

"You have thought of lots of things to worry about, haven't you?" Jodie said. "But think for a minute about what you have done by putting together this plan. Amelia is taking a trip across Canada when this time three months ago she hadn't left home for thirty years."

"But I'm taking her away from you guys."

"Raymond and the twins are showing more independence and courage than we ever would have thought possible. You have given Zac and me an opportunity to do something for Amelia for a change. We can hold down the fort and give her a chance to get away for a few weeks."

"But what about Amelia?" Rachel asked. "Do you think she is just doing this for me, or do you think she really wants to go?"

"I think she wants to go," Jodie answered. "She's going to get to visit Jason and his family. She's going to get to live her dream of having tea at the Empress Hotel. Of course she's going for you, but she must want to do this for herself, too, or she wouldn't be doing it."

"What about my grandmother and my father?" Rachel said, fidgeting with a string hanging off of her T-shirt. "Am I just fooling myself to think I am going to find this perfect family waiting for me? I'm sure my dad isn't instantly going to become Father of the Year as soon as he sees me."

Jodie leaned over and squeezed Rachel's shoulders. "You're giving your father something more to motivate his recovery. You're allowing your grandmother and aunts a chance to meet a part of their family that has been missing. You don't have to do anything but let yourself enjoy the trip. No one can tell you how it will work out, but you can be proud of doing your part. Amelia will be driving back no matter how your visit goes. Just go and let whatever happens, happen."

Rachel laid her head on Jodie's shoulder and together they watched the crimson ball of the sun setting over the lake.

The Jimmy was packed and everyone was sitting in the kitchen having a special good-bye breakfast. Jodie had made waffles and Zac had cooked ham drenched in maple syrup. Amelia was compiling long lists for them and bobbing up and down out of her chair like a yo-yo. "The twins have a dentist appointment on July 11. Don't forget to check for potato bugs as the plants get bigger. Look under the leaves for the eggs; you have to get those, not just the hard-shelled adults."

"Amelia," Jodie broke in authoritatively. "We are no stranger to the Colorado potato beetle and besides, I think you put that on at least two of our lists." Jodie dropped a waffle on her plate and gave her a quick hug. "Sit still and eat."

Rachel was putting the last few items in the cooler. "It looks like we have enough food here for the whole trip!" she laughed.

"Buy enough bread at the market on Saturdays to do the week," Amelia continued. "Don't try to make the bread, Jodie. You'll have enough to do trying to feed this bunch without trying to make bread."

"Maybe I'll make it," Zac said. "I expect I'll be eating most of my meals here." He rubbed the top of Raymond's head. "Someone has to help this guy run this funny farm."

"I'm going to call every night, no matter where we are," Amelia rambled on. "If I don't get a hold of you I'll leave a message. You can always call my cell phone if you need to for any reason. Dr. Hollway's number is by the phone."

"Don't worry so much, Amelia," Zac said as he led her

toward the open door. "We'll be fine. We will look forward to hearing about your travels every night. Now get in the Jimmy and get going!"

Amelia pulled the Jimmy up to the gas pumps at the Irving station in Welsford. Rachel got out and started filling up the tank. The station attendant began washing the windshield.

"Where are you ladies headed on this beautiful day?" he asked.

"We're driving across Canada," Rachel replied.

"Get out of town!" he said.

"That's what we're doing," laughed Amelia as she went in to pay for the gas.

"So it's just you and your grandmother driving all the way across the country?" the attendant asked Rachel as they waited for Amelia to return.

"Yep!" Rachel didn't bother to correct the man. She just reached into the backseat, grabbed an apple from the cooler, and refastened her seatbelt.

Amelia did most of the talking during the first three hours of the drive. She spouted all the New Brunswick trivia she could muster and kept the conversation going with only a few words from Rachel. They stopped briefly to look at the Hartland covered bridge and Amelia told Rachel that the bridge had been opened on July 4, 1901, and it was 1,282 feet long. But the last hour of the drive was tortuous. The upbeat feeling Rachel had felt when they left this morning was not what she felt now. All she wanted was to be home at the lake.

Finally Amelia turned the car off the highway and headed into the driveway of the hotel they'd booked for the night, called the Happy Club Motel. *Maybe a place with "happy club" in its name will perk me up,* Rachel thought to herself as Amelia got out of the car to check them in.

The woman behind the counter was very pleasant, but Amelia thought she seemed to linger too long staring at the bumps on her face. The woman asked her a bunch of simple registration questions, things like her name, how many guests were in her party, her street address and postal code. But the answers were stuck in Amelia's throat as if she were being asked to bare her soul. Her license plate number? She had no idea. Credit card? She didn't have a credit card. She had never needed one. Maybe she should have gotten one before taking this trip. She was going to pay with cash. She finally got the key for room 10 from the woman and hurried out to get Rachel and the suitcases.

"The first motel was built in 1925 in San Luis Obispo, California," Amelia said as she and Rachel dropped their bags on the floor of the hotel room. "It was called the Mo-tel Inn. Mo-tel was an abbreviation of motor and hotel."

"Let's take a walk and find somewhere to eat supper," she continued. "I'm stiff from driving all day. I haven't sat still that long for years. I'll get used to it after a few days, I suppose. We'll drive longer tomorrow, and we'll stop on the other side of Montreal tomorrow night."

The phone rang six times before Jodie answered it.

"I was just taking the clothes off the line when I heard the phone ringing," she told Rachel. "Peter Totten dropped off three piglets today and Zac and Raymond are working on a yard for them so the pigs can come in and out of the shed. Crystal and Chelsea have hardly left the pig shed. They've named the piglets Lavendar, Lilac, and Larry, but Zac and Raymond are calling them Breakfast, Lunch, and Supper."

The twins got on the phone and talked to Amelia and then Rachel spoke to Jodie again before they hung up the phone. Rachel's feeling of homesickness was even stronger than it had been earlier and she wished she was back home in her own room, not in a room at the Happy Club Motel. She picked up the TV remote and started scrolling through the channel guide, looking for something to take her mind off where she was and where she was heading.

It was a beautiful sunny day and the air was already hot when they exited the Tim Horton's drive-thru at seven o'clock. Amelia had wanted to get an early start on a long day of driving. The thought of driving through Montreal was worrying her a lot—all that traffic and the numerous road changes were a lot to handle, especially for someone who hadn't driven through a city in over thirty years. She kept telling herself she'd be fine—she was just going to take her time and follow the map that Jodie had printed off for her. Montreal would probably be the biggest challenge of the whole drive and at least she would get that over with at the start of the trip.

Rachel tore a piece off her bagel and took a bite. She had dreamed about her father last night. In the dream he was walking ahead of her in a field and she couldn't see his face. She was trying to catch up with him, but he just kept walking faster. She tried calling his name, but the sound of her voice was lost in the wind and she couldn't get his attention. She had woken up around four o'clock in the morning and laid awake for a long while afterwards, trying to get the dream off her mind.

"The province of Quebec is three times the size of France." Amelia's voice broke into Rachel's reverie and brought her back to the present.

"My parents were never married," Rachel said. "Garnham was my mom's last name, and her mom disowned her when she had me. How can a mother disown her own kid? She hated my father. The first time I ever saw my mom's mother was at the funeral. I wanted to ask her that day if she wanted to own my mother again now that she was dead. I was hoping she didn't want to own me, but I didn't have to worry about that."

Rachel stared out the window and wiped the tears that were slowly dripping down her cheeks. She had forgotten all about that and wondered why it had come to mind now.

"My parents weren't married either," Amelia said. "I don't even know who my father was. My grandmother raised me. The last time I saw my mother I was about ten years old. She used to visit once or twice a year, but when I was ten she just stopped coming."

"I wonder how big the pigs will be when we get home," Rachel said, deliberately trying to change the subject. "The raspberries will be ready when we get back, won't they?"

"Yes, probably," Amelia answered. "We usually have raspberries by the end of July. We should make sure we get a good meat and vegetable meal at suppertime tonight. And let's try to find a hotel with a pool so you can go for a swim."

They drove on chatting about harmless topics—chickens, sunflowers, the garden—until they stopped for lunch. They said nothing more about mothers or grandmothers.

The traffic through Montreal took all of Amelia's attention.

She gripped the wheel tightly as she navigated through the busy highways. As soon as they got out of the most congested area, Amelia pulled over and laid her head down on the steering wheel.

"In 1910, the magician Harry Houdini was the first solo pilot to fly a plane in Australia," she said after a few minutes. "He taught himself to drive an automobile just so he could drive out to the airfield and then he never drove again."

After checking into the motel Rachel and Amelia ate supper at the restaurant next door and then called home. Everyone took turns talking to them. Amelia described the horror of driving through Montreal to Zac and he asked Rachel afterwards how she'd managed as the passenger. Jodie told them that she'd cooked the first of the peas for supper and raved about how good the hot milk cake that Chelsea made for dessert had been. Raymond told them that he and Zac had picked up a field of hay at the Fullertons' this afternoon and they still had to unload the wagon. Then he played his newly learned rendition of "Stairway to Heaven" on the guitar as Amelia held the phone out so that Rachel could hear it, too. Crystal told Rachel she'd put a doll's bonnet on one of the pigs and took its picture.

After they hung up the phone, Rachel and Amelia headed down to the pool. It was just a small one, with the deep end only being five feet, but it felt wonderful to them both to be swimming again. Rachel counted her laps as she swam the length of the pool. She promised herself she'd make it to twenty. Each time she started underwater she pretended she was plunging into the lake. Amelia finished her quick swim and bundled up on a lounge chair on the pool deck to read while she waited for Rachel to finish.

"I only have two laps left, Amelia," Rachel called out.

Rachel pulled herself up out of the water and wrapped herself in the scratchy hotel towel, thinking about the long day she and Amelia had ahead of them tomorrow. *After my long swim, maybe I'll sleep soundly tonight*, she thought as she followed Amelia to their room. *I hope my dreams are of fresh peas, haylofts, and pigs wearing bonnets.*

"Cows and cornfields have a home within Ottawa's city limits at the 1,200-acre Central Experimental Farm," Amelia shared as she and Rachel filled up a bag with cobs of corn from one of the stands at the ByWard Market in Ottawa. After spending most of the afternoon at the Canadian War Museum, they were now strolling the aisles at the market to pick up some food for dinner.

Once they paid for their corn, Rachel and Amelia headed back to the Jimmy. Their plan was to drive a little bit longer and then find a motel to stop at for the night. On their way out of the city, they drove by the Chateau Laurier, one of the most expensive hotels in Ottawa. As they passed the hotel's grand entrance, Amelia said, "I guess we won't be staying there. They probably wouldn't let us cook our corn in one of their fancy suites."

About an hour later they pulled into the entryway of the Colonial Fireside Inn in Pembroke. They were able to get a room with kitchen facilities, so they checked in and cooked their corn in a big pot on the tiny hotel-room stove. Once it was finished, they carried it outside to eat at a nearby picnic table.

"This corn isn't as good as the stuff we grew last year," Rachel commented, buttering her third piece. "By the time we get home, ours will just be getting ripe, won't it?"

Home. Rachel liked the sound of that. It was still surprising to her that she felt so settled at Amelia's. She thought of how homesick she was now, how much she wanted to be back at the farm, swimming, cooking, and even weeding the garden. Every other time that she'd felt homesick in the past five years it had been for her old house on Regent Street. The feelings had always been wrapped up with the deep sadness she felt, the longing for her mother and her brother, and the awful pit of shame she kept pushed down so she wouldn't have to think about it. But today her thoughts of home had taken her to the end of Walton Lake Road. They took her to her room up over the kitchen and to the smells of food cooking on the wood stove. They took her to the lake, its sights and sounds clear in her mind.

"What was your mother's name, Amelia?" Rachel wasn't sure what had made her ask that or why it even mattered.

"Her name was Vivian," Amelia answered.

Rachel said nothing more, taking the pause and the look on Amelia's face as an indication that she did not want to say anything more about her mother. Rachel was sorry she had asked the question. She started hulling and cutting up the strawberries, filling two Styrofoam cups.

"My mother was beautiful," Amelia continued after a few minutes of silence. "Every time she came to the farm she was dressed in fancy clothes and her hair and makeup were perfect. She would usually drive up with some strange man we had never seen before and she never stayed very long. It was as if she was afraid she would get dirty or her hair would get out of place. She would sometimes stay for a meal, and I always insisted on serving her, trying to impress her with my grown-up ways. But she never seemed to notice me at all. The visits always ended the same way: she would ask Gram for money and leave in a hurry, giving me a quick hug before taking off. I always stood there wishing she would take me with her, or at least stay longer."

"Is your mother still alive?" Rachel asked hesitantly.

"I don't think so, but I really don't know," Amelia answered. "The last time we saw her was September 1964. She just disappeared after that. My grandmother tried for years to find her, but as far as I know she never did. I gave up the thought of ever seeing her again years ago. She was never a mother to me in any sense of the word, but it took me a long time to come to terms with that."

Rachel didn't know what to say to Amelia. It must have been terrible not knowing where your mother was and feeling like she never cared enough about you to stay and look after you. At least she had always known her own mother had loved her. Her mom had always taken good care of her and Caleb. And above everything else, Rachel knew her mother had not left her on purpose. She knew what had taken her mother away from her, and she knew it was all her fault.

It was raining as Rachel and Amelia left Pembroke early the next morning. They stopped at a grocery store to replenish their cooler with lunch and snack foods, and then headed toward Sault Ste. Marie. Rachel was determined to keep the conversation away from serious stuff today, and it seemed like Amelia was thinking the same thing. They spent the morning talking about trivial things, and as usual Amelia punctuated their chat with random facts whenever she could: Neil Armstrong stepped on the moon with his left foot first. An average four-year-old asks 437 questions a day. Napoleon Bonaparte constructed his battle plans in a sandbox. If you attempted to count stars in the galaxy at a rate of one every second, it would take around 3,000 years to count them all.

After their conversation died out, they occupied their time by playing a game of finding all the letters of the alphabet in order on signs on the side of the highway. X and Z were the hardest ones to find.

Around one o'clock, they stopped at the Big Nickel monument in Sudbury. They walked around the giant coin and took some pictures of themselves in front of it, and then found a grassy spot to sit down and eat their lunch. About an hour later, they packed up their cooler and got back in the car for another long drive.

Both Rachel and Amelia remained fairly quiet on the long stretch of highway that afternoon. At around seven o'clock they finally rolled into Sault Ste. Marie, where they checked into the Skyline Motel and then headed straight to Swiss Chalet for supper. After dinner they called home, and then turned on the TV. By the end of their third episode of *Golden Girls*, both Rachel and Amelia were fast asleep in their beds.

The next morning's drive seemed longer than usual to Rachel because there wasn't much to see except for trees, rocks, and water. She and Amelia stopped at Obatanga Provincial Park around two o'clock for a late lunch. They ate by a large lake, and despite the swarm of mosquitoes hovering overhead, Rachel changed into her bathing suit and went for a quick swim. She ran right in and swam out over her head and back in again several times. Burnfield Lake was beautiful, but it felt nothing like her lake.

The afternoon drive seemed to go by quicker, and Rachel and Amelia were in good spirits when they arrived in Marathon around suppertime. They bought Chinese take-out at Wok with Chow Restaurant and took it to their room in the Travelodge Motel, moving quickly as the woman at the desk had told them to watch out for bears. They called home, left a message when no one answered, and went to bed early.

The next afternoon Rachel and Amelia stopped at the Terry Fox Monument outside of Thunder Bay. They asked someone to take their picture as they stood beside the monument, pointing at the New Brunswick crest. Then they drove on to Ignace, where they settled into a small room at the Trading Post Motel.

Rachel and Amelia entered the lobby of the Winnipeg View Motel to register for their room. The woman behind the counter stared rudely at Amelia's face, obviously horrified.

"Is that contagious?" she asked loudly.

"No," Amelia responded calmly. "I have Neurofibromatosis. It's not infectious. It's caused by a mutated gene."

Amelia filled in the hotel registration form, not showing that the woman's insensitive remark had bothered her at all, then took the room key and walked away quickly.

"We are in the middle of the country, and the middle of the continent as well," Amelia told Rachel as they carried their suitcases up the stairs to their room. "Winnipeg has many claims to fame. Monty Hall, the host of the game show 'Let's Make a Deal,' was born in Winnipeg. Winnie-the-Pooh was named after Winnipeg by a Canadian lieutenant in the Fort Garry Horse Militia. And Winnipeg is the Slurpee capital of the world. The citizens of this city consume 400,000 Slurpees a month, even during the cold winter months—and Winnipeg has some of the coldest weather in the country!"

Rachel could see that Amelia's frenzied recitation of Winnipeg trivia was covering what she was really feeling. "That woman was very mean to ask you that," she said as they stepped into their room on the second floor. "It was very rude."

"I could say that I'm used to that reaction," Amelia said, putting her suitcase down and turning around to face Rachel. "But of course I'm not, since I chose to hole up for thirty years and not let anyone see my face."

"You should have asked to speak to her boss. She had no business asking you that."

"When I was young I had light brown spots on my face and nobody knew why. My grandmother had never seen anyone else with them and the doctor had no idea what caused them. If I got them from a parent it must have been the father I never knew, because my mother certainly never had anything like them on her face. I remember staring at them and wondering if that was why my mother didn't want me. She was so beautiful and I thought she probably couldn't stand to have such an ugly daughter. When I became a teenager people started telling me I was pretty. My friends would tell me I should be a model or an actress. I had never been told that before and I became obsessed with my looks. I started wearing makeup to cover the brown spots and I was always fixing my hair and fussing over my clothes. I got more and more caught up in how I looked. Then there was the Miss Saint John pageant. All my friends kept telling me that if I won, it would be the springboard to a modeling career. By that time I had already finished my social work degree and was happily working at the Protestant Orphans Home in Saint John, but I entered the competition, vainly believing what my friends were telling me. I won and that just made me more obsessed with my looks."

Rachel propped herself up on the bed, putting two pillows behind her head, while Amelia continued to talk.

"I was engaged once, you know. I met a very nice young

man named Sheldon in university and we dated for a few months. He proposed to me on the night before the pageant, surprising me with a beautiful diamond ring. I was caught up in the whirlwind of the whole thing and was sure that he only loved me for my looks, because deep down I felt like he didn't even really know me. I had never taken him to meet my grandmother and hadn't told him anything about my mother. After I won the title of Miss Saint John, I was so full of myself that I didn't even see that this was a problem. Then Gram got sick and I had to go home to take care of her for a few weeks. During that time, my condition began to get worse. The brown blotches on my face started turning into clusters of bumps that I couldn't conceal with makeup. I pushed all my friends away and wouldn't take Sheldon's calls when he tried to reach me. After it became clear that the bumps were not going away, I finally called him and told him that I didn't love him and that I wouldn't marry him. I mailed the diamond ring back to him, and after a few weeks he gave up trying to talk to me. My friends quickly forgot me and I put all my energies into looking after Gram until she died about a year later. Then I called my boss and asked if it would be possible to take in foster children. By that time the orphanage had closed and there were lots of kids who needed homes." Amelia stood up and straightened out her clothes, then walked over to the sink and washed her face. "But that's enough about that," she said as she picked up a towel to dry off. "Let's call room service and order something really delicious for supper. Pass me the menu in that folder on the bedside table, would you?"

The prairie landscape was so much different than the rugged terrain of Ontario. As they travelled down the flat open highways, Rachel and Amelia both felt the excitement of getting closer to their destination. They were going to stay at Jason and Megan's in Calgary for five days and then head on to Golden.

After registering at the Super 8 motel in Regina and taking their suitcases into their room, Rachel and Amelia went to a nearby A&W restaurant and ordered takeout before heading back to the room to call Jodie and the kids.

The phone call home was upsetting for Amelia. Jodie told her that the night before, Chelsea had woken up from a nightmare and it had taken a really long time to calm her down. She had been hysterical and had cried violently for a long time, constantly asking for Amelia. In her disturbed state she couldn't grasp the fact that Amelia wasn't there, and Jodie had been worried she would make herself sick with her crying. Seeing her sister like that had of course upset Crystal, and Jodie had needed to call Zac to come and help comfort them.

"I should never have left them," Amelia told Rachel after she hung up the phone. "Chelsea hasn't had a bad night for quite a while, but I should have known that if she did she would need me to be there. When they first came to Walton Lake, we went through that almost every night. Sometimes both of them would wake up at the same time, but even if it was just one of them, the other would always wake up and panic when she heard the other. For months they wouldn't let me touch them, and they'd go crazy if I tried. I'd have to let them exhaust themselves before I could get anywhere near them. It took such a long time to gain their trust."

"In my first foster home I woke up the second night from a very scary dream," Rachel said. "I was screaming uncontrollably and the woman came in and told me to shut up. Her husband had to get up early for work the next morning and she told me if I woke him up she would give me something to scream about. After that, whenever I had a bad dream I would put my head under my pillow and quietly calm myself. The dreams finally stopped and I never told anyone about them. The twins were lucky to have you. Try not to worry. They'll be okay until you get home. They know you're coming back and they have Jodie and Zac there until you do."

Chapter 8
Silence is Golden

After filling themselves at the motel's breakfast buffet, Rachel and Amelia started out for Calgary. They figured that if they drove straight through, with only a bathroom stop or two along the way, they should get to Jason's about suppertime. The night before Amelia had Googled Jason's address on the computer in the hotel lobby and made a printout of the directions for how to get there from the highway. She'd called Jason and he'd said that he and Megan would have supper ready when she and Rachel arrived. He'd seemed really anxious to see them. Rachel had called Audrey Anderson, as well, and she had also sounded excited that Rachel was getting so close.

Two bathroom stops and a quick lunch at a roadside rest stop put Rachel and Amelia on the Macleod Trail in Calgary at quarter after five. After only a few wrong turns, they drove up to Jason's house at 56 Millcrest Green at quarter to six. Jason ran out to meet them with Logan running along behind him.

"Hi, Amelia!" he said excitedly as he helped Amelia out of

the truck and gave her a big hug. "I can't believe you're here. Meg has supper all ready."

"You must be the famous Rachel," Jason said. "You're the wonder worker who persuaded Amelia to take off driving across the country. I don't know how you did it, but we're very glad you did. The last thing I ever hoped for was to have Amelia come to visit. I may not let her go, now that she's here. We could use some help with that little namesake of hers—she's keeping us up around the clock! Come on in and meet my girls. We can bring your stuff in later."

By the time supper was finished Logan had made Rachel his new best friend. After dinner he kept her busy playing with his Thomas the Tank Engine toys and reading his two favourite Curious George books over and over. He was not happy when his mom said it was time for bed, but when Rachel promised to still be here when he woke up in the morning, he gave in. Amelia had been holding the sleeping baby Amelia in her arms for most of the evening and decided after the long day that she, too, would go to bed.

Rachel was going to sleep on the pull-out couch in the family room. Jason put Logan's toys away and set out her bedding for her. "There's a shower stall and towels and such in the little bathroom down here," he told her as he headed up the stairs to his room. "Let me know if there's anything else you need. Have a good night."

Rachel made up her bed then headed to the bathroom for a shower. She stood in the shower for a long time, letting the water wash over her as she thought about the day's events. Jason and Megan had both been so nice to her and had made her feel really welcome. Logan was absolutely adorable, and baby Amelia was precious. It felt so nice being here with them, feeling almost like part of their family. She hoped that she would feel this way when she met the Andersons.

The next day was a frenzy of activity and it went by very quickly. It was late in the evening now, and Amelia, Megan, and the kids had gone to bed. Rachel and Jason were sitting together in the family room, watching an old episode of *Law and Order* on TV.

"I bet it was the lawyer," Jason said. "Megan gets mad at me when we watch this show because I always guess who committed the murder in the first ten minutes. Have you seen this one before?"

"No," Rachel answered. "We don't watch much TV at Amelia's. There's always something else to do. Lots of chores and stuff, and we play a lot of games after supper."

"Dominoes, right? We played that a lot when I lived there too. Does Zac still think he's the champion?"

"Yep," Rachel laughed. "He does this little victory dance when he wins."

"Oh, I remember that dance. And how about the two rules?" Jason asked. "Are they still the same? *Do your part* and *spend an hour alone at the lake*."

"Exactly," Rachel answered. "Still the same."

"I thought that the lake rule was the stupidest thing I had ever heard when I first got there. I was ready to break all the rules, just for the sake of breaking them. But how do you break a rule like that? Go for twenty minutes instead of an hour, stay for two hours, or refuse to go at all?"

Rachel laughed, thinking about the first time she'd walked down the hill to the lake, and what she'd thought of the rule back then.

"I think that's part of Amelia's magic," Jason continued.

"She never backs kids into a corner with rigid rules."

"Did Amelia have Sam and Bud when you lived there?" Rachel asked.

"Yep," Jason said, smiling. "I miss those old dogs. And I miss that hour alone at the lake, too. I know it sounds pretty extreme, but the lake saved me. It saved me from the fate I was sure was mine." He lowered the volume on the TV and turned toward Rachel. "Did Amelia tell you anything about me?"

"No," Rachel said, fiddling with the fringe of a blanket hanging over the back of the couch. "She doesn't tell us much about the other kids. And she doesn't make us talk about stuff we don't want to, either. That is one of the best things about her, I think."

"Well, there definitely was a time I didn't talk about my past, but I talk about it now. I decide if and when people need to know about it and I don't feel the shame about it that I once did. My father murdered my mother."

Rachel looked over at the commercial playing on the TV. She stared at the talking hamburger, not wanting to look at Jason. She hoped the shock of his words didn't show on her face.

"I was eleven years old," Jason continued. "I saw my mother bleed to death while my father turned on the hockey game and drank a beer, cheering his team on as if it were a normal Saturday night. After the game was over, he called my uncle and told him to call the police. Then he took off and left me alone in the house with her. They arrested him at a bar later that night. He killed himself in his jail cell five months later."

Rachel turned to face Jason, unable to keep the tears from filling her eyes. She couldn't understand how he could be so calm about all this. He was telling her this horrible thing as if they were discussing the plot of a movie or TV show, but it had all actually happened to him.

"I didn't talk for weeks afterwards," Jason said. "I thought

129

I was just as guilty as he was because I hadn't called anyone for help. I'd just sat there on the kitchen floor across from her body and watched her take her last breath. I was sure that I was just like him, that I was just as evil and heartless. I thought I was dangerous, that I should be locked up so I couldn't hurt anybody, but no matter how hard I tried to convince people of that they wouldn't believe me. It wasn't until I was in my fourth foster home, when I gave the man who ran it a broken nose, that they finally locked me up. That was right before they brought me to Amelia."

"You thought it was *your* fault?" Rachel asked, not understanding how he could possibly blame himself for something he'd had no control over.

"I knew I hadn't killed her," Jason explained. "I loved my mother and I was a good kid, but I had always been told I was just like my dad. That night those words took on a whole new meaning. I thought if I was just like him, I must be capable of doing what he had just done."

Rachel wanted to say something, but the words froze in her throat.

"Walton Lake. I remember getting left there and being told I had to spend an hour by myself beside the lake. Two weeks before getting to Amelia's I had been locked up in a juvenile facility with no freedom at all. But now all of a sudden I was being left all alone. I knew I could take off if I wanted to. I could just follow the shoreline back to the road and take off. But when I went to the lake, I heard a sound that stopped me in my tracks. It haunted me and I just sat down on the shore and cried. I cried like a baby. I can't explain why, but it felt as if my mother were there with me. I know it sounds corny, but that's what it felt like. It felt like she was there with me, telling me I was a good boy and that this place was where I needed to be."

Jason kept talking. Rachel pushed back a falling tear in awed silence. "The sound was a loon. There was a pair nesting on the lake, and I became obsessed with them. I read everything I could about the common loon. That summer I read somewhere that loons mate for life, and even though I've since read information that disputes that fact, back then I believed it and held the whole species in reverence. I spent all of my hours at the lake watching that pair. The male was loyal to the female, and they were both protective of their young. They never left their babies alone."

"I've seen loons at the lake," Rachel said, finally finding her voice. "Would they be the same ones?"

"The life span of the common loon is between twenty-five and thirty years, and they generally come back to the same place every year, so it probably is the same pair if nothing has happened to either one of them."

"That's amazing," Rachel said. "They have two young ones this year."

"They just lay two eggs. The young will fly off before the lake freezes. Every day when I went to the lake that first summer, I would talk to my mother and tell her that I was going to be a father and a husband just like the male loon. And it seemed like the loons could hear my thoughts. They would swim in close to me and every sound they made was like they were talking right to me. They're what got me through that first summer. Little by little, it broke my anger and fear down. That's why I say the lake saved me."

"I love the lake too," Rachel said, her eyes shining. "Zac taught me to swim last summer. I would never try before, but the first time I saw that lake I knew I needed to swim in it."

Talk about being corny, Rachel thought to herself. She had almost just told Jason that she'd believed right from the start that the lake was the place to hold her tears. She barely even knew him. She wiped her eyes with her shirtsleeve and turned back toward the TV.

"I told you it was the lawyer that killed her," Jason said. "What can I say? It's a gift." He stood up and headed up the stairs to bed.

Rachel sat there alone, listening to the muffled voices coming from the TV. She thought about what Jason had told her about his parents and how normal he seemed now with his wife and kids. She wished her dad had been able to be that kind of father to her and Caleb. *Maybe it isn't too late for him,* she thought. *I guess in a few days I'll find out.*

Amelia and Rachel sat on lounge chairs on the front lawn as Jason finished packing the Jimmy for them. Their five days in Calgary had gone by so quickly. Their plan to meet Jason, Megan, and the kids in Jasper on the way back home was the only thing making their departure easier.

The drive from Calgary to Golden would only take a few hours, so they were going to have enough time to stop at Lake Louise and Banff on their way. Rachel had talked to her grandmother last night and she could hardly believe the day had actually come when she would meet her.

Rachel had really wanted to talk to Jodie and Zac last night, but Mrs. Fullerton had answered the phone when she and Amelia had called. She'd been babysitting Raymond and the twins because Zac and Jodie had gone out for dinner and a movie with Roger and Leslie. Rachel had been really disappointed that she'd didn't get to talk to them—she'd been counting on them being able to help calm the nerves that were building inside her as the time to meet her family approached.

A few minutes later, Rachel and Amelia backed out of the

driveway. As they rolled down the windows to wave good-bye, they heard the pleading cries of Logan, who wanted to know why he couldn't go with Nanny Amelia and Aunt Rachel.

Lake Louise was amazing. Standing on the boardwalk, looking at the snow-covered peaks rising up above the sparkling blue lake, Rachel felt a strong sense of peace and thankfulness.

Amelia pointed over toward Chateau Lake Louise, a huge hotel perched grandly on the edge of the lake. "Look at the golden windows," she said. The sun was shining off the expanse of windows facing the lake, making them glow with golden light. "My grandmother once told me a story about a house with golden windows. Every day a little girl who lived in a poor part of town would look up at a large mansion up on the hill above where she lived, and when the sun shone a certain way, it would make the windows in that mansion appear golden. The little girl would always stare up at that house with the golden windows, dreaming of someday living there. When she grew up, she became wealthy, and her new circumstances allowed her to finally live the dream of buying that mansion. When she moved in, she looked down at the small house she had grown up in, and the way the sun was shining on it made it look like it, too, had golden windows. My grandmother always followed that story with the quote: 'Truth, like gold, is to be obtained not by its growth, but by washing away from it, all that is not gold.'"

Rachel wondered if there would be any truth for her in Golden, BC, if she would drive through these beautiful mountains and find a place and a family that would wash away the tarnished parts of her past.

Wildlife
Livestock
Broken Pavement
Horseback Riders
Avalanche
Falling Rocks
Rocks on Road
Wildfire
Trucks Turning
Curves
Blasting
Road Construction
One Lane Bridge
Elk
Bighorn Sheep
Stock at Large
Watch for Crime
Wind Gusts

Rachel and Amelia passed eighteen signs of warning as they drove through the mountains toward Golden. For some reason she couldn't explain, Rachel had started writing them down as they appeared on the roadside. It seemed comical to her that the road held such dangers. Beneath her list, she wrote a few signs of her own for the road they were taking:

Caution
Family Ahead
Watch for Disappointment
Broken Promises

"Did you ever try to find out who your father was?" she asked as she closed her notebook.

"No, not really," Amelia answered. "It never seemed that important to me. I guess I put all my energy into thinking about my mother. She was such a mystery to me and I had magnified her in my mind. It was my mother's love I craved, not my father's. And the more I craved it, the more I blamed and hated myself for not getting it from her. I never blamed her. In my mind, she was perfect. I thought I was the damaged one. I think I am only just now coming to terms with the falseness of that."

"What if my dad and I are damaged?" Rachel asked. "Too damaged to deserve anything better?"

"I doubt that either one of you are as damaged as you have convinced yourselves," Amelia said, looking over at Rachel. "Take it from me: most of the beliefs in our shortcomings are spoken much louder from within than from anyone else."

As they rounded a curve in the road and headed down the steep decline, the town of Golden came into view. Whatever dangers or pitfalls were ahead, Rachel was finally coming to the place she had been obsessing about for months.

Rachel and Amelia drove down the tree-lined cul-de-sac and pulled into the driveway of a cedar-shingled bungalow. Before they even had time to get out of the Jimmy, what seemed like a never-ending stream of people of all ages filed out the front door of the house.

One woman rushed toward Rachel and before she said a word Rachel knew it was her grandmother. Audrey Anderson extended her arms, and without even thinking about it, Rachel allowed herself to be enfolded into her grandmother's embrace.

When she finally let Rachel go, Audrey had tears streaming down her cheeks. "You are just as beautiful as your picture," she said. "I've dreamed of this day for fourteen years. I can't believe I am finally meeting you!" Then, turning toward Amelia, she added, "I can't thank you enough for bringing my granddaughter to us, Miss Walton."

"You're very welcome," Amelia responded. "But, please, call me Amelia. And there's no need to thank me. I'm very happy to be here, but it was Rachel's determination that made this trip happen."

A tall man with shoulder-length hair and a short beard edged his way through the others standing on the front lawn. He wiped the tears from his cheek and approached Rachel, waiting for her to make eye contact with him.

"Hi," was all he said.

Rachel knew who this must be, but she just nodded her head. She couldn't bring herself to give the father who'd abandoned her so many years ago much more than this.

"She's beautiful, Donald," a young woman who was very pregnant said as she walked up beside them. "I'm your Aunt Victoria," she told Rachel, giving her a hug.

"Happy Birthday, Rachel," Donald said as he awkwardly moved closer and gave Rachel a quick hug.

"My birthday is actually tomorrow," Rachel said blankly.

"I know. You were born on July 15, 1996, at six-thirty in the morning."

Rachel stared at Donald, not knowing what to say. He may have been there when she was born, but that didn't mean her knew her. He knew nothing about who she was, and spouting out her birth details didn't get him off the hook for not being around for the rest of her fourteen years.

"Let's go into the house," Audrey called out to everyone. "Rachel, we're having your birthday dinner tonight. The food is all laid out—there's enough of it to feed an army! We'll make all of the introductions inside."

The eighteen people who made up the welcoming committee were quickly categorized and introduced to Rachel and Amelia when they entered the house: Rachel's dad, Donald; his girlfriend, Penny; Patricia, her husband, Tom, and two little boys, Elliot and Liam; Victoria and her husband, Malcolm; Great Aunt Alice, her daughter, Janet, and Janet's three kids, Chad, Emily, and Stephen; Audrey's best friend, Ruth Shannon, and neighbours Owen and Winnie Johnston; another neighbour named Laura Mac Dougall; and, of course Audrey, who everyone seemed to be calling Nanny A.

Everyone headed straight for the kitchen. The table, the countertop, and the stovetop were covered with heaping dishes of food. After instructions from Audrey, everyone began to line up and start filling their plates. Penny passed Rachel a plate and motioned for her get in line, and Donald followed behind them. Rachel filled her plate, trying in her mind to put the names and faces of her new family in place.

After supper, Audrey carried out a huge birthday cake with "Happy Birthday, Rachel!" written on it in orange icing, and everyone sang the birthday song. Rachel blew out the candles. The wish that came immediately to mind was for all of her new family members to like her. She carefully cut the cake, passing the slices to her Aunt Patricia, who topped each one with a scoop of ice cream.

Once everyone finished their cake, Audrey and Ruth headed to the kitchen to clean up. Amelia and Rachel offered to help, but were told to join the others outside and relax. Amelia sat on the porch swing beside Winnie and Laura, and was quickly caught up in their friendly chatter. Rachel sat down on the back step to watch the older kids and some of the grown-ups playing a game of washer toss.

Donald came over and sat on the step beside her. They sat, not saying anything, for a few minutes before Donald finally broke the silence. "Do you want to take a walk?"

Rachel looked around, hoping that someone else would want to come with them. Taking a walk with this perfect stranger, even if he was technically her father, was not something she wanted to do. It wasn't like they were going to catch up on the last fourteen years of their lives over a twenty-minute walk. Even if they could, she wasn't even sure she wanted to get to know him.

She didn't know what to say, so she got up and followed Donald as he led her down a trail towards the woods. After walking for a long time without speaking a word, Rachel and Donald came up to a small wooden bridge. A sign nearby told Rachel it was called the Kicking Horse Pedestrian Bridge.

"I helped build this bridge in 2001," Donald told her, stopping in the middle of the bridge and leaning against the railing to look down at the stream below. "It's a timber-framed Burr Arch design. I was sober and clean for the month I was working on it. I was saving money to go back to New Brunswick when I finished, to try to convince your mother to take me back. It didn't work out that way, though. I got into the cocaine real bad and all I could think of was how I was going to get my next line."

"Mom used to tell us that you would be back when you got better," Rachel said, taking a place beside Donald. She could see the rocks glistening in the streambed below as she leaned out over the railing. "She said that when you got better you would be a good father to us."

"That was very generous of her," Donald said. "It makes it sound like I chose to leave so that I could get better. The truth was she kicked me out and I didn't go easy. She always said that you kids came first and she wouldn't let anything hurt you or your brother. There was no way she would let me be around you guys as long as I was using. All those years when she was raising you alone she knew that I wasn't making any effort to get clean and I know things weren't easy for her."

Rachel started walking again. When she reached the end of the bridge, she sat down on a concrete slab that sloped toward the riverbank. Donald caught up to her and sat next to her.

"This bridge doesn't actually go anywhere," he said. "There isn't much to see when you cross it. The town is planning on developing this area to make it more appealing to tourists. I like it the way it is, though. I walk here a lot. It was on one of my walks here that I finally convinced myself I was ready to make a change in the way I was living."

"How did Mom meet you?" Rachel asked.

"In the nineties I travelled all around the country, building post-and-beam timber structures. In 1995, I was building a big hunting lodge in the Miramichi. One Friday night after work, a few of my buddies and I headed to Fredericton for dinner and some drinks. We ended up at a place called the Diplomat Restaurant, and your mom was our waitress. For me, it was love at first sight. Though when I used to tell that to your mom she always said it was a miracle that I could even see that first night, I was so drunk. She wouldn't give me the time of day that first night, so I sobered up and came back the next night and asked her to go to the Hilltop Pub with me when she got off work. She wouldn't go then, either. But I came back every weekend for the next few weeks, and finally my charm won her over. When the hunting lodge was finished a short time later, I got a job in Fredericton working for a local contractor so I could be closer to her. A couple of months later, she got pregnant with you. We were both really excited to have a baby, but I was an asshole and was drinking a lot and getting into some drugs. I spent all of my money on booze and drugs, and your mom had to keep working right up until she gave birth. After you were born, I smartened up for almost a year. I kept asking her to marry me, but she wouldn't. She said that when I was sober and clean for two years she would consider it. Then she got pregnant again. I didn't make the two-year point, but she put up with me until after Caleb was born. I was so messed up by that point that she had to tell me to leave. I didn't take that very well and she finally had to get a restraining order against me."

"What were you doing that was so bad she had to get a restraining order?" Rachel asked. "Did you ever hurt her?"

"I almost did once," Donald said quietly, focusing on his feet as he dug a hole in the dirt with the toe of his boot. "I kicked the door open to her apartment one night when I was really wasted. I was going to make her take me back, no matter what I had to do, and God knows what I would have done. But when I got through the door, you were there, crying and hanging onto her leg. You were wearing a fuzzy pink housecoat and your hair was still wet from your bath. I remember freezing in my tracks, thinking what a monster I was to make my baby girl so afraid of me. I turned around and left. The next day I headed back out west. Your mom was kind enough to write to me every once in a while, though she always made it clear that as long as I was drinking or doing any drugs she did not want anything to do with me."

"I remember that housecoat,' Rachel said. "The sleeves were up to my elbows when Mom made me stop wearing it. I used to sleep with it after that."

Donald stood up and turned toward the bridge. "I should get back to Mom's now," he said, heading back up across the bridge. "I only get day passes from the centre, so I have to be back every night at ten, and it's a long drive to get there. I only have one more month of that, though, and then I start getting week passes so I only have to check in on weekends. After that I go to full discharge, with just a weekly counseling session. It's great that you're staying for a whole week. Penny and I want to take you hiking and maybe even white-water rafting, if you're up for it. I've been with Penny for almost a year. She's like your mom: she won't take any shit from me." He paused and turned back to her, giving her a shy smile. "I wish I could have done this years ago. Your mom deserved so much better. So did you, Rachel."

Audrey greeted Rachel the next morning as she entered the kitchen. "Happy Birthday! How about just you and I go out to breakfast? We have a diner downtown that makes the best French toast ever."

"Sounds good," Rachel answered. "Where's Amelia? She's usually up with the sun."

"She's gone to see Ruth's vegetable garden. Yesterday Ruth was telling her about the raised bed garden she planted, but it isn't anywhere near as big as the one you've got growing, from the sounds of it. I would love to hear all about Amelia's farm. I grew up on a farm in Saskatchewan, you know."

"Really?" Rachel said as she pulled her sandals on and followed her grandmother outside. "That's so cool. I saw a whole bunch of farms when we drove through Saskatchewan, but they didn't look anything like ours."

Audrey and Rachel talked nonstop as they walked to the Eagle's Eye Diner.

Rachel and her grandmother spent their hour at the diner lost in conversation. Audrey did most of the talking, though she was interrupted here and there by people stopping by the table to say hello. It seemed everyone in Golden knew Audrey Anderson. She proudly introduced Rachel to everyone who spoke to them as they sat and ate their breakfast.

"I have been so concerned about you, Rachel," Audrey said as she picked up her cup of coffee and took a sip. "I know it must seem like none of us have given you a thought, especially since your mom and Caleb died. You must have felt so alone. I am so sorry I didn't find you sooner. I hope you believe me when I say I have thought of you every day since you were born."

Rachel didn't know what to say. Looking at this woman— her grandmother—she couldn't seem to muster the anger she thought she should feel. She felt that anger towards her mother's mom, who could have been the family she had needed, but had chosen not to. But for Audrey, who had been separated from her by distance and circumstance, all she felt was a desire to get to know her.

"I thought we might go shopping for a bit before we head home," Audrey continued. "I have always wanted to buy clothes for my only granddaughter. I know they won't be the pink frilly things I used to dream of, but I would love to buy you something you would like."

"That would be nice," Rachel said, soaking up the leftover syrup on her plate with her last bite of French toast and popping it in her mouth. "I'd like that."

Rachel had surprised herself by trying on several outfits and letting her grandmother buy her two pairs of jeans, three shirts, and a new bathing suit.

"She wants me to call her Nan," Rachel told Amelia as she showed off each purchase. It was after lunch, and they were sitting together in the spare room in Audrey's house. "She introduced me to everyone she saw, and most of the people we talked to already knew she had a granddaughter in New Brunswick."

"Oh, that's lovely!" Amelia exclaimed as Rachel showed off her new orange T-shirt.

"She grew up on a farm," Rachel continued. "Her father had dairy cows. She used to have to help milk them by hand before they got milking machines."

Amelia smiled as Rachel told her all her all about Audrey's life on the farm. "Maybe you'll try to milk our cow when we get home," Amelia interrupted, "now that you know the skill runs in the family."

Rachel stared through the car window up at the Top of the World Ranch treatment centre as Penny pulled into a parking spot. Donald had come out to Audrey's yesterday, too, but this was the first time Rachel had come along for the drive to pick him up for the day. She had imagined this place so many times since reading her grandmother's letter, and now she was here. She had pictured herself pulling up and seeing her father sitting on a bench, waiting for her. Her imagination had made him look like Brad Pitt and the facility look like the ranch on a TV show she sometimes watched when she lived at the Harriets'. But seeing the facility now, first hand, it was nothing like she'd imagined—it was just a large log building set among some trees, with some small cabins scattered around it. It certainly didn't look like the type of resort ranch she'd pictured. The idea of her father's addiction and his struggle to get sober was somehow more real now that she'd seen this place, and him, with her own eyes.

"Let's take Rachel to Huckleberry's for breakfast," Donald said to Penny as he got into the car. "She needs a good meal to give her enough energy to make it through what we have planned for her today."

Rachel was the third person back on the left side of the big blue raft. She pulled the strap tighter on her helmet, trying to take in all that the guide was telling them. "If you fall out of the raft…" she heard the guide say before she panicked and tuned the voice out.

What have I gotten myself into? she thought as she tried to mentally glue her butt to the bottom of the inflatable raft.

"I've never lost anyone yet!" the guide told everyone with a laugh.

There's a first time for everything, Rachel thought to herself.

The guide went through the commands and each of the raft's occupants moved their oars in the manner instructed. The command "hold on" was the one that worried Rachel the most. Apparently if the guide called "hold on!" they had to grab a rope that was threaded through the metal loops running down the centre of the raft and try not to fall out. *This dinky little rope is supposed to keep me from falling out and bashing myself on the rocks?* Rachel thought. *Not likely.*

She braced herself as the guide pushed the raft into the river and jumped on. She looked over at her father and Penny, who had already started paddling, obviously old pros at this. As she checked her life jacket one last time to make sure it was done up tightly, Donald turned back toward her and gave her a wink. "Don't worry," he called. "You're gonna do great!"

"It was amazing!" Rachel told Zac over the phone later that afternoon. "The worst rapid was called the Shotgun. I thought I was going out on that one, but I didn't! Can you believe I even did it? Last year at this time I wouldn't even go in the water in a wading pool, and now I've conquered the Shotgun! I would love to do it again, but I know it's really expensive. Donald and Penny bought my picture, too. The company is going to mail it to me later."

Rachel talked to Zac for a few minutes longer before repeating the whole story to Jodie, who was seriously impressed. Then she told a shortened version to Raymond and then to both of the girls. By the time she got off the phone, she was exhausted, so she headed for a quick nap before dinner. As she laid down on the futon in Audrey's den, she thought about all the fun she'd had today. It was the first day since she'd left Walton Lake that she hadn't felt homesick. It was great talking to Zac and the other kids, but for once when she spoke to them she didn't wish she was back there with them. She was happy here, in Golden, BC, with her grandmother and her father and the rest of her real family.

"Nan and I are going to get a few groceries," Rachel told Amelia on Saturday after lunch. "I'm going to help her make her world-famous BBQ ribs and potato salad for supper tonight."

"Would you like to come with us, Amelia?" Audrey asked.

"No, you two go ahead," Amelia answered. "I'm going to go next door and help Winnie pick some of her green beans, deadhead her roses, and do some baking to get ready for the people who are checking in tomorrow. I've been getting lazy on this trip and need to get my hands in the dirt and myself in the kitchen."

As she and Audrey drove to the grocery store, Rachel noticed that the middle school was just three blocks from her grandmother's house. *If I lived here I could walk to school*, she thought.

"Did Dad go to that school?" Rachel asked.

"No," said Audrey as she made a left turn and headed in toward town. "When your dad was in middle school we lived in Vernon. We moved here when he was 16. Sometimes I blame the move for his problems. He had a hard time fitting in when we came here and got in with some bad kids. His dad died that year and it wasn't easy for him." There was a minute of awkward silence before Audrey spoke again. "I'm sorry. I don't have to tell you that, do I, sweetie? You know all about how hard it is to lose someone. I can't even imagine how hard it has been for you. You are wonderful girl and I know your mom would be very proud of you."

Rachel was glad when they reached the parking lot and she could jump out of the car. *A wonderful girl*, she thought. *Yeah right. If she knew the truth, she wouldn't think I was wonderful, or that anybody could be proud of me.*

Yesterday Rachel, Donald, Penny, Amelia, and Audrey had hiked the trail to Sherbrooke Lake. The climb had been quite steep and challenging, but it was all worth it when they reached the lake. The sight of the blue-green water surrounded by the rocky brown mountains was absolutely breathtaking. Penny had taken tons of pictures and had even printed the one of Rachel and her father standing in the doorway of the Paget Peak fire lookout off for her when they'd got back last night. It was the first picture she'd ever had of her and her father, aside from the wrinkled hospital picture he had sent her. The two of them had spent every one of the last six days together—six days, trying to catch up on fourteen years.

Today everyone was just hanging around at Audrey's. It

was a hot day, and Audrey had filled a small kiddie pool for Liam and Elliot. Tom had started the barbecue for supper. Amelia and Ruth were sitting together on some folding chairs, talking about gardening.

Rachel and Donald were out on their second walk of the day. The hike to Kicking Horse Bridge had become a daily routine that provided them with some time alone. Donald usually did most of the talking, but Rachel was starting to be more open about things that she had never imagined sharing with anyone, let alone a father she hadn't known for most of the last fourteen years. They were walking across the bridge, talking about yesterday's hike, when Donald spoke the words that Rachel had read in her father's letter a few months ago, words that she hoped he would never say out loud: "I thank God every single day that you didn't die in that accident."

Rachel stopped walking and turned away from her father. She took a deep breath, trying to come up with a topic that would divert the conversation away from the one thing she couldn't bear to talk about. The words were stuck way down in her throat and all she could feel was an erupting anger, a rage she was sure she couldn't mask. She walked on, pretending she hadn't heard what her father had said, hoping her silence might keep him from saying anything more about the accident.

Donald put his hand on her shoulder. "Rachel, I know it must be hard…" he started. The last words of his sentence were clipped with the rising emotion.

"Don't talk to me about the accident!" Rachel shouted. "Don't even pretend you have any idea what happened! You have no idea. You weren't there. You were too busy getting drunk or stoned. Too busy living your own life to worry about a wife and two kids."

Donald removed his hand from her shoulder and walked

around to face her, leaving a good space between them. "I know, Rachel," he said quietly. "I am so sorry I wasn't there."

"Do you even know what happened?" Rachel spat venomously. "They both died instantly. Some guy drove through a red light and rammed into them. The car was demolished and they both died instantly. That's what people kept telling me afterwards. They thought that if they kept telling me that, it would make me feel better. 'Your mother and brother died instantly. They didn't suffer.' Perfect strangers told me that."

Donald moved closer, trying to wrap his arms around his daughter. Rachel pushed him away, tears streaming down her face. "I wasn't with them!" she yelled. "It wasn't some turn of fate that kept me alive. It wasn't some wonderful miracle. I wasn't with them."

"Sometimes it's hard to understand why things happen, Rachel," Donald said calmly.

"i was supposed to be with them!" Rachel screamed these words. She leaned up against the timber railing of the bridge, her body trembling, and looked down at the water rushing below her. The thing that she'd been pushing down inside her, the pain and guilt she'd been avoiding for years, was clawing its way up and coming out. After a few minutes, she spoke again, but quietly this time. "I was having a stupid temper tantrum because Mom said she couldn't afford to pay for swimming lessons. I ran outside, climbed the tree in the backyard, and told her I wasn't going. You know, I don't even remember where she was going. I just remember I refused to come down from the tree. Finally she and Caleb had to leave without me—she was late for her appointment and she said she would deal with me when she got home."

Rachel was now shaking uncontrollably, her words coming slowly between the wrenching sobs. "They never came home. I made her late. If I had gotten in the car when she'd told me to, she wouldn't have been there to get hit by that car. That guy would have hit someone else, or nobody at all. But she and Caleb were there when he sped through that light because of me. It's my fault they are dead. It's *my* fault. *My fault.*"

It was clear to everyone when Donald and Rachel walked back into the yard that something was wrong. Donald had his arm around Rachel, supporting her. Her face was red and blotchy and she had obviously been crying. Donald asked Amelia to follow him as he led Rachel into the house. They took her into the den and closed the door.

Donald lifted his arm off Rachel's shoulders and she fell into Amelia's embrace.

Amelia eased Rachel down onto the futon and covered her with a brightly patterned afghan. Donald sat down on the floor beside her, brushed her hair off her forehead, and wiped the tears from her face with a tissue. Amelia sat down in a chair across the room and watched as Rachel allowed herself to drift off to the welcome escape of sleep.

Once Rachel had fallen asleep, Donald told Amelia what had happened back at the bridge.

"She vomited after she told me," Donald said. "It was like she had a poison inside her and had to get it out. She's been blaming herself for their deaths for six years. She kept her guilt bottled up all that time, and never told anybody. I told her it wasn't her fault, but I know from experience it doesn't do any good for someone else to tell you stuff like that. You have to be ready to forgive yourself. God, I hope she is ready to forgive herself."

Chapter 9
The Coast is Clear

Rachel didn't wake up until the next morning. She vaguely remembered hearing Penny come in sometime in the dark to wake Donald up from where he had fallen asleep on the floor beside her. He had kissed her cheek before heading back to the centre for the night.

Rachel changed out of yesterday's clothes and took a long shower. When she was finished, she walked into the kitchen. Amelia and Audrey were sitting at the table, drinking their morning coffee.

Audrey stood up and gave Rachel a big hug, trying to keep herself from crying. "God love you, you poor darling," she said. "It breaks my heart to think what you've been through. I feel so guilty for not being there for you. Thank God you came to live with Amelia."

Rachel had been worried about what her grandmother and the others were thinking, now that they'd found out about the details of the accident. She was afraid that they'd blame her for it, the way she blamed herself. Her father and Amelia had been very comforting, but she wondered if the rest of the family would be as understanding.

"It wasn't your fault, sweetheart," Audrey told her now, as if she could read what Rachel was thinking. "You were seven years old. You did *not* cause that accident. You have to let the guilt go, Rachel. Your mother would never have wanted you to blame yourself. You haven't had anyone to tell you that, but you do now, and all the people here who love you will not let you carry that burden any longer."

Just then, Donald and Penny entered the kitchen through the back door. They went straight for Rachel and wrapped their arms around her, hugging her for a long time.

Amelia carried a fresh pot of coffee over to the kitchen table as the others sat down.

"Rachel," Audrey said slowly, "there's something that we'd like to speak with you about. We've all had such a wonderful time getting to know you over the last week, and it breaks our hearts to think about you leaving. We can't bear to lose you, now that we've finally found you." She put her coffee down and took Rachel's hand. "We would like you to think about staying here permanently, about living with us."

"I'm going to let you all discuss this privately," Amelia said, standing up. "This is a conversation for you four to have. I'll go next door and visit with Winnie for a bit. Rachel, you can come find me when you're done, if you want."

Rachel nodded at Amelia and watched as she walked out of the room. She picked up her toast and took a small bite, not able to look up at her father, Penny, or her grandmother. She wasn't sure she wanted to hear what they were going to say, even if it was what she had secretly hoped for since getting her first letter from Audrey.

"Penny and I are going to get married when I'm done the program," Donald said. "I'll move into her place, and we would love to have you live with us, Rachel. Until then, you could live here with Mom."

"You're welcome to live here as long as you want to," Audrey chimed in. "You know I would love to have you in Golden, Rachel, but it has to be your decision. I know you want to go to Victoria with Amelia so she can have tea at the Empress. You could still do that. We thought that we could meet up with you in Jasper when you hook up with Jason and his family, and we're hoping that by that time you can let us know what you have decided. We know it would be a big change for you to move here, and we want you to have time to think it over. It's too bad we're so far away from New Brunswick, but if you stay here we can fly you out there next summer so you can see Amelia and your friends."

"I want to be a dad to you, Rachel," Donald told her. "I hope you'll let me try. Better late than never. Right?"

Rachel found Amelia sitting in Winnie's backyard. She repeated the conversation she'd just had with Donald, Penny, and Audrey almost word for word. When she was done talking, Amelia leaned over and wrapped her arms around Rachel. Both of them were overwhelmed with the mix of emotions they were feeling.

"The national orchestra of Monaco has more individuals in it than its army," Amelia said, straightening up and looking into Rachel's tear-filled eyes.

"I've missed your valuable snippets of information over the last few days, Amelia," Rachel said.

Amelia smiled at Rachel. "It's been nice to visit with your grandmother and everyone. They seem like good people, and they certainly are taken with you."

"Yeah, go figure."

"I know it's a lot to think about, being part of a new family. But really you have always been a part of them; it just took a while for things to come together."

"I'm happy that they want me to live here," Rachel said, "but what about you? I don't want you to feel like I'm not grateful or that I don't want to live with you anymore."

"This isn't about me, Rachel," Amelia answered. "All I have ever wanted for you, for any of my kids, is a place you can be safe, a place where you can find yourself, a place you can call home. When home can be another place, whether it happens now or when you are grown up and ready for a family of your own, I am more than happy to see you embrace that."

Rachel and Amelia stood on the wide sidewalk, staring up at the massive building. Colourful flowers edged the grounds, ready to welcome them. The large white letters that read "The Empress" looked like they were growing right out of the green vines that covered the building's façade.

"I can't believe I'm about to have high tea at the Empress Hotel!" Amelia squealed giddily. "I was eight years old when I first saw a picture of this place in a *National Geographic* magazine. I've been dreaming of doing this ever since that day. Thank you so much for bringing me here!"

Rachel laughed. "You drove, Amelia."

"That's all I did," Amelia said, smiling. "You, my girl, did the rest."

Rachel gave Amelia a big hug and together they walked up the steps, through the doors, and into the hotel's elegant lobby.

The maitre d' seated them at a square mahogany table under one of the large windows. A server arrived almost immediately and placed fine bone china teacups and saucers in front of them. She returned shortly thereafter with a beautiful silver tea service, steaming with what she told them was Earl Grey tea. Then she placed a three-tiered china plate filled with fancy-looking food on the middle of the table, pointing as she described each of the different types of sandwiches on the first tier. "Cucumber; BC salmon and cream cheese; shrimp mousse with fresh papaya; carrot, ginger, and cream cheese; and curried mango and chicken salad."

Rachel listened to the descriptions, not exactly sure of all the ingredients. She was determined to try them all, whatever they were, because they looked so fancy and also because this was Amelia's day and she was going to enjoy every minute of it.

The second tier held four currant scones with dishes of clotted cream and strawberry preserves. The bottom tier was packed with sweets that the server described as checkerboard cake with marzipan, miniature chocolate éclairs, lemon tarts, chocolate truffles, and Earl Grey shortbread cookies.

Amelia and Rachel took their time working through the tiers, savouring every bite and every moment in this beautiful place.

Amelia and Rachel were waiting in line to catch the ferry back to Vancouver. The plan was to drive straight through to Jasper and meet Jason and Megan at the Jasper Inn that night. Then Donald, Penny, and Audrey would meet up with them the next day.

"I'm going to have to make up my mind by tomorrow, Amelia," Rachel said, watching the cars rolling onto the ferry in front of them. "I don't know how I'm possibly going to do that. I'm really afraid that I'll make the wrong decision."

"Fear is a funny thing, Rachel," Amelia said. "Sometimes the things we think will scare us the most don't scare us at all. You know, all those years I spent pent-up at Walton

Lake I was never afraid of being alone. I was never afraid of anything I had to deal with on the farm. I was never afraid of storms or hard winters. And I was never afraid of any of the troubled kids who came to me. All I was ever afraid of was not being good enough, not being deserving enough. I let that fear cripple me and keep me in not just a physical place, but a place in my head that tied me to that fear." She turned toward Rachel. "Don't let that fear be what makes up your mind. You are deserving of being just who you are and right now you have the choice of doing that in two different places. The choice you make does not bind you. You have a home with us and a home with Audrey, Donald, and Penny. You can change your mind anytime. You are deserving of love, and the most important place that love comes from is within yourself."

A shrill ringing noise interrupted their conversation. The sound was so unfamiliar that it took them a couple of seconds to realize that it was Amelia's cell phone. When Amelia answered, she heard Jodie's excited voice on the other end.

"We're engaged, Amelia! Zac and I are engaged. He asked me to marry him! I know that you're probably surprised. It surprised us, too, when we realized our friendship had turned into love. He is so amazing, but I don't have to tell you that, Amelia. Hurry up and get home. We have a wedding to plan!"

"I'm over the moon!" replied Amelia. "I couldn't have picked anyone better for you or for him. I must admit, though, that I'm not totally surprised. If wishing for something makes it come true, I have certainly been wishing for exactly this for a long time. Tell Zac he is a smart man and I am very proud of him."

When the ferry attendant motioned for Amelia to drive down the ramp into the underbelly of the big boat, she passed the phone to Rachel.

"I want you to be my maid of honour, Rachel," Jodie told her. "And tell Amelia she'd better be ready to give me away. We're getting married beside the lake next July, as long as that's okay with Amelia, of course. You will be in our wedding, won't you? No matter where you choose to live, you have to be here for our wedding!"

"Of course I will be in your wedding, Jodie," Rachel answered. "I am so happy for you guys! We just got on the boat. We're on our way home—I'll see you soon!"

Rachel and Amelia sat not speaking for a few minutes in the parked car until Rachel broke the silence. "I love you, Amelia. From the first day I came to live with you, you've made me feel like I belonged. I've been homesick ever since we left Walton Lake and I can't wait to see Zac and Jodie. I miss Raymond and the twins, too. I just want to go home. I know Dad, Penny, and Audrey are my family, and I'm really glad they want me to live there, but I want to go home with you."

Amelia turned toward Rachel, tears streaming down her face. "I love you too, Rachel," she said. "I didn't even want to think about having to head home without you. Jodie and Zac were really worried you would stay. Raymond was freaking out on the phone last night and Chelsea told me not to let you stay. Crystal said she would let you have the biggest pig if you came home. But it had to be your choice, Rachel. If your choice is to come back home to Walton Lake, you need to know that we are all very happy about that." She leaned across the centre console and gave Rachel a big hug. "In 1947, the Flying Wallendas perfected the seven-person pyramid on a wire thirty-five feet above ground. If they could pull that off, surely the seven of us can take our places, keep our footing steady, and work together to keep one another from falling."

Chapter 10

Sugar Cubes, Spiders, and Sword Fights

"According to Roger, it hasn't rained on July 7 for 35 years," Jodie said as she stood looking out the kitchen window at the overcast sky. "Today's his birthday, and apparently it's always been sunny for his birthday. He even checked it out on the internet. But by the look of those clouds, this July 7 could be the exception to that rule."

"Rain on your wedding day is supposed to be good luck," Amelia said. "But the CBC said it was going to be hot and sunny today, so hopefully you'll get your wedding luck a different way. A spider in the wedding dress also brings good luck. I'm sure we could get Raymond to get one of those big-bellied spiders from the chicken shed and slip it down the back of your dress if you want to be sure the sun will shine."

"Finnish brides go house to house with pillowcases, receiving gifts from neighbours," Amelia continued with her wedding facts. "In Greek culture, the bride puts a sugar cube in her glove. They say it will sweeten the union."

"I'm not wearing gloves, Amelia."

"Do you want to know why the bride stands on the left of the groom?" Amelia asked Rachel as she entered the kitchen.

"You know she is going to tell you whether you want to know or not," Jodie teased. "But at least all her trivia is helping me stay grounded. I am losing my mind trying to remember all of the stuff I need to do today! The cheesecakes need to come out of the freezer. The caterer will be here soon and I need to tell her how I want the tables set up. I don't know what we'll do if it rains. The hairstylist is going to be here at ten to do everybody's hair. I'll go wake up the twins, and then I have to go get a shower." She headed up the stairs toward the twins' room.

"Moroccan woman take a bath in milk the night before their wedding to purify themselves," Amelia called behind her.

"Oh, if only I had known that last night, Amelia!" Jodie called down jokingly. "You can't be keeping important information like that from me. Now Zac is going to have to marry a bride who hasn't soaked herself in a tub full of milk. He'll have to settle for one that has only cleansed herself with Body Butter Coconut Scrub. Do you think there's enough dairy in that?"

Amelia turned to Rachel. "The bride standing on the left side of the groom dates back to the days when the groom would have to kidnap his bride and fight off other men who also wanted her. He would hold the bride back with his left hand so his right hand would be free to use his sword."

"I'm glad that's not the case anymore," Rachel laughed. "I'm not sure how good Zac is with a sword!"

"Check it out," Raymond said as he headed down the stairs in his tuxedo. He had grown at least a foot in the last year and hardly looked like the same kid. "I'm James Bond!"

"You are one good-looking guy," Rachel said, flattening down the lapel on his jacket. "Now get out of here. Roger is in the yard waiting to take you to Zac's. The photographer is taking pictures there first. Don't get all wrinkled."

Zac had made the decision to wear tuxedos for the wedding when he, Roger, and Raymond had gone looking for dress clothes a few weeks ago. "I only plan on doing this once, and I'm going to dress the part," he'd said. Since Jason couldn't be there to try one on, he'd sent the measurements for his tux. Luckily when they went to pick them up yesterday Jason's had fit him, but Raymond's had needed to be altered since he'd lost more weight and gotten taller since the first fitting. Roger had picked the new one up for him this morning.

"Well, we can't let the girls get all the attention!" Raymond said, bounding out the door with a huge grin on his face.

Donald, Penny, and Audrey had arrived at Walton Lake a week ago. They'd driven a camper trailer across the country and were staying at the lake for the entire month of July. At the end of the month, Rachel was going to stand up at her dad and Penny's marriage in front of the Justice of the Peace. They didn't want to take away from the wedding they had come to help celebrate, but they'd really wanted Rachel to be there when they became husband and wife.

It had been really difficult for Rachel to tell her father and grandmother that she had decided to go back to New Brunswick with Amelia, but in the year that had followed they'd all worked really hard at building strong relationships. Every Sunday night Donald would call from Golden and Rachel would talk to every single member of the family, even Aunt Victoria's new baby, who couldn't even talk yet.

Jason, Megan, Logan, and little Amelia were here. too. They

were staying at the Amsterdam Inn for the wedding weekend, since things were so crowded at Amelia's, but Amelia had insisted they stay at the farm for the rest of their visit.

The sun shone brightly in the afternoon sky. A warm breeze swept over the guests as Sam and Bud led them down the path toward the lake. Zac, Raymond, Roger, and Jason got out of Roger's car and walked by the house quickly so Zac wouldn't be tempted to look in and try to get a glimpse of his bride. They took their places beside Reverend Stephenson in the arbour that Roger and Zac had constructed and carefully put in place along the shore early this morning. Bud bounded back up the hill to accompany Chelsea and Crystal as they walked down to the lake, hand in hand, in matching yellow dresses. Their pretty red curls were swept up and crowned with strings of daisies. Rachel followed behind them wearing a long lavender dress, which matched the beautiful bouquet of pansies she clutched between her hands.

Rachel looked at the small crowd sitting in front of her. Behind them, the wide expanse of her beloved lake was framed with dark green trees. She remembered back to her first days standing at this lake. In those days she had thought she was all alone, with no family. She'd been sure no one loved her. But now she could see Penny, Donald, and Audrey in the crowd in front of her, dabbing their eyes with tissues as they watched her walk toward them. She heard a loon cry and she looked at Jason, who smiled back at her. She thought about how he had come to this same place and had felt the same way. She turned her gaze to Raymond, who was standing tall and handsome, with such pride in his face. She saw Chelsea standing a distance away from her sister, holding baby Amelia. Crystal was sitting on the ground cross-legged with Bud's shaggy head in her lap. She looked at Zac and watched his face light up as Jodie appeared on the hill behind her.

Rachel took her place beside the arbor and turned to watch as Jodie and Amelia made their way down the path. They both kicked off their fancy shoes and headed down barefoot, arm in arm. When they got to the arbour, Amelia kissed Jodie's cheek, hugged Zac, and stepped away.

Amelia sat just behind Rachel as the ceremony began. Rachel's mind was not on the words the minister was speaking. She was thinking instead of how it was that Amelia had brought them all together to this place. This farm at the end of the Walton Lake Road, which had been in some ways a prison for Amelia, was a place where some of the scared, sad kids that she had taken in had found freedom.

Here she was at the lake she loved with Amelia, Jodie, Zac, Raymond, Chelsea, Crystal, Jason, Megan, Logan, little Amelia, Dad, Penny, and Nan—her family, the people she loved and who loved her. Rachel looked at the blue water and thought about going for a swim as soon as she could get out of this fancy dress. She kicked off her tight shoes and felt the sand between her bare toes.

At the same time, Sam dropped his stick at Zac's feet. With his eyes still fixed on his beautiful bride, Zac bent to pick it up. He raised it high above his head and threw it into the water. Everyone watched as Sam bounded in after it, knowing that one of them would be the person Sam would take his treasure to next.

Acknowledgements

Thanks first to Terrilee Bulger and Acorn Press who have brought *Ten Thousand Truths* to fruition. I am thankful every day that she believed in the words of my first manuscript and had the vision to see it as a book and continues to support and encourage my writing.

Thank you to Caitlin Drake who worked with me to shape the story. Always a pleasure to take that journey with you, Caitlin.

Thanks to my friend Kathy who drove with me across this glorious country of ours having some of the experiences Amelia and Rachel had taking the same trip. We did not get to the Empress Hotel but we did have a great pulled pork sandwich at the Burnt Toast Café in Whitehorse.

This book holds a piece of my great Aunt Alice who was very much like the character Amelia and nurtured me with good cooking and love in the house I brought Rachel to. This house which unfortunately is empty and falling down, now only holding apple crates and memories is a mansion in my mind and heart. It was wonderful to spend a year visiting it again in my imagination as I wrote this story.

I am one of the world's hugest Anne of Green Gable fans and hold Lucy Maud Montgomery in high esteem. Rachel is my Anne Shirley and Amelia Walton my Marilla Cuthbert. I applaud the author's determination and tenacity and feel honoured to join her in the ranks of Atlantic Canada authors. May some young reader care about Rachel Garnham as much as I cared about Lucy Maud Montgomery's famous red headed character.

To my husband Burton who continues to be my best friend and biggest fan. (Yes, Mrs. White has another book he is going to make you buy.)